PRAISE FOR **BROKEN RECORDS**
SPOTLIGHT, BOOK ONE

"TOP PICK! This excellent take on the celebrity-and-normal-person romance moves at a fast clip while satisfying at every turn."

—*RT Book Reviews*

"Hollywood style meets Nashville charm in this sweet, sexy fling turned romance."

—*Publishers Weekly*

PRAISE FOR **BURNING TRACKS**
SPOTLIGHT, BOOK TWO

"FOUR STARS… *Burning Tracks* is a deeply emotional work that explores love, loss, risk and the struggles of commitment and self-sabotage. In the first book, readers were introduced to a new love, but in this book, readers observe an established relationship. This makes *Burning Tracks* fundamentally different read [sic] from its predecessor, both in tone and in what's at stake for our heroines."

—*RT Book Reviews*

PRAISE FOR **BLENDED NOTES**
SPOTLIGHT, BOOK THREE

"A witty, touching, nuanced—and very sexy—romance."

—*Kirkus Reviews*

PRAISE FOR *Spice*

"… Compl   ying romantic plot is
the perfect   n and Benji, who are
bound to i   a at its best!"

—*RT Book Reviews*

"Suzanne keeps the humor warm and the sex real."

—*Publishers Weekly*

PRAISE FOR PIVOT-*and*-SLIP

"4.5 stars… Balancing laughter with touching emotions, this novella is a great first effort."

—*Carly's Book Reviews Blog*

JILTED

lilah
suzanne

interlude ✦✦ **press**™ • new york

interlude 🧩 press • new york

"What is straight? A line can be straight, or a street, but the human heart, oh, no, it's curved like a road through mountains."

—Tennessee Williams, *A Streetcar Named Desire*

PROLOGUE

SOMETHING ISN'T RIGHT.

Link fidgets with the hem of their skirt and twists the satiny, pleated fabric between shaking fingers. Cold feet have become a full-body chill, and Link regrets choosing the thin skirt as wedding attire. The air conditioning is set to subzero in this quaint boutique hotel, which isn't helping, and the skirt is not doing much to hide Link's trembling legs. At least the vintage tuxedo jacket is non-breathable polyester, something Link never thought they'd be thankful for.

Across the altar, the officiant clears her throat. She checks her watch and glances down the aisle; concern pulls at her thick eyebrows. Link can't remember her name; they'd picked the first officiant that sounded okay, same as everything else in order to expedite the whole wedding thing. It had seemed so important to get it all done quickly, but what was the hurry, really? It hasn't even been a year since Link has known Jamie, and she's been such a chameleon in that time—changing jobs, hair, clothing styles, interests, friends. Link found it intriguing, exciting. Link wonders now, for the first time, if that's an unstable place to start a marriage.

The crowd begins to mumble; people shift in their chairs to look back at the doors that remain closed. Cold panic courses through Link. Something isn't right.

Looking for reassurance, Link scans the front row to their mother, Danielle, who is dressed in bright, clashing layers of draped chiffon and has long ribbons twisted into her double black-gray braids. She looks like a tropical bird. Danielle casts a meaningful look that seems to say: *You really should have let me do a sage cleansing of the space first* or *Jamie is a Capricorn; you know what that means.* Link has always had Danielle's support, no matter what. That doesn't mean the support is never grudging or without an occasional *told ya so*. Well, she's wrong about Jamie, and this wedding will prove it.

Jaime is running late. That's all. The plan was to walk up the aisle together to "Rainbow Connection," but Jamie's sister told Link to go ahead and wait at the altar, and so Link is here, and Jamie isn't. Did she change her mind about not being walked down the aisle? Is it too late to go back and get her? Link finds Eli and other friends in the restless crowd. Eli, positive and loyal and steadfast, sends Link an encouraging, double thumbs-up.

Finally, the wooden doors are flung open, and Jamie appears, a vision in vintage pink and purple tulle and matching pink and purple hair. Everyone stands. Jamie begins to come up the aisle, but, instead of relief or joy, Link's icy-cold feeling of dread turns to a heavy block of ice in their gut. Something isn't right. Before Link can sort out why, someone else flings the doors open.

Jamie stops and turns around. "Matt? You came!"

The guy is handsome, square-jawed, and put together in a way that suggests an exclusive country club membership. He's someone Jamie's clearly familiar with and fond of, yet his whole presence is at odds with the Jamie Link knows—if they really know her at all.

"Jamie, I have never stopped loving you and came to win you back," Matt says, without even a tremble in his voice.

Before Link can process the declaration of love between the person Link is supposed to marry and *someone else*, she's gone, a floating specter of pink and purple running off hand in hand with whoever the hell this Matt is, and Link—Link has not stopped clinging, white-knuckled, to the sides of their skirt. The cold dread is gone, replaced by shock and humiliation.

Danielle was right. Never trust a Capricorn.

ONE

"Go. Be happy."

Love is sacrifice, or so claimed the vows that Carter had planned to say at his own wedding next year. Instead, his fiancé is now off with his true love, the one that got away, the one that is not Carter. And Carter, standing in the interior courtyard of this beautiful historic hotel all alone instead of being whisked off on an impulsive romantic getaway weekend the way he'd thought, is noble or selfless—or a complete and total jackass.

Carter reviews the events that led him here, mentally cataloging the moments and hoping to lock them away and never think of them again. Matthew received a wedding invitation from an ex approximately three weeks ago. Short notice according to the guidelines from wedding planning experts, Carter thought at the time, but he was otherwise unbothered by the invitation. Yet Matthew seemed unusually agitated about what Carter incorrectly assumed to be the frustrating lack of time to plan a trip. He and Matthew then got into another disagreement about where and when to hold their own wedding. There were other steps to fill in on the wedding planning agenda, and so Carter let it go, figuring they'd sort it out eventually. Neither of them was in much of a hurry.

He forgot about the invitation altogether and, when Matthew suggested a trip to New Orleans, Carter assumed it was a romantic trip for the two of them—also incorrect. Though not usually a nervous flyer, Matthew was extremely agitated on the plane, and Carter's recitation of flying safety statistics only seemed to aggravate him further. Of course,

Carter's compulsive need to recite information seems to aggravate most people, so again he didn't think much of it.

At the hotel, Matthew led them both on a frenzied search for *something* as Carter's luggage banged into his shin and his travel pillow remained looped around his neck. The old French Quarter hotel was bursting with fascinating architectural details that Carter barely had time to take in. Matthew finally stopped at this interior courtyard, where a small group of people in fancy clothes and updos waited just outside carved cypress doors and whispered furtively amongst themselves. The wedding party, he realizes now, or part of it, heading inside to where the ceremony was taking place. If *she* was with that group Carter didn't notice, too distracted by lavender-flowered wisteria vines spilling over high brick walls and potted dahlias in pops of yellow and red and orange on the pale stone floor beneath skinny trees. Hedges in the center were carved into a small labyrinth, and, in the center of that, a fountain trickled sun-speckled water. Birds chattered. Matthew said he needed to tell Carter something. Thinking Matthew was irritated that Carter had stopped to ask a member of the housekeeping staff whether the acanthus molding on the fireplace was carved or cast in plaster, Carter struggled to make sense of Matthew's expression: he looked pained, yet flush with excitement.

Then Matthew confessed he'd come to stop the wedding and win back a long-lost love. Carter was so surprised that, at first, he was only relieved Matthew wasn't annoyed with him. Such a strange reaction, Carter thinks now, *relief* at finding out his fiancé is in love with someone else. Practically speaking, though, what choice did Carter have but to let him go? He'd come all that way, after all. Noble, it seemed at the time.

Love is sacrifice? What a load of garbage.

The beautiful stone fountain in the courtyard burbles gently. Carter stands motionless before it, tracks the flow of clear water from spout to basin, over and over, and does not feel angry and does not feel sad and does not feel betrayed. Carter watches the water flow until he doesn't feel anything at all.

Without even a room to crash in, so poorly thought out was his now-ex-fiancé's eleventh-hour secret-true-love's quest, Carter has been hauling his luggage around with nowhere to go and no plan to get home. He leaves his things at the front desk and feels significantly less burdened. There are no rooms available at this hotel, but he can have a drink at the small bar off the lobby and figure out what to do next without worrying about where to put his travel pillow.

The architecture is entrancing; the hotel has a classic French Creole style unique to New Orleans. He's never been to The Big Easy—and isn't here in the best of circumstances—but, between the fascinating architecture, the jubilant jazz band playing in the bar, the invigorating mint julep in his hand, and his well-honed skill at crushing his feelings into nothing more than a small, cold pit in his stomach, Carter is downright excited when he sits at the hotel bar.

"Laissez les bon temps roulez," he says to the bartender and lifts the glass in salute. The bartender moves away. Carter takes a long swig of his drink and sets it down with a refreshed "*ahh.*" He knocks on the weathered, sepia wood of the bar. "Isn't this salvaged Louisiana cypress? Nice."

The bartender is ignoring him. Carter shrugs, sways on his barstool to scan the bar for more interesting details, and finds the person next to him slumped facedown on the bar. Long wavy black hair obscures their face, and they're wearing a white satin skirt and a purple tuxedo jacket. A flower pinned to the jacket has been crushed against the lip of the bar. A single petal falls from the flower and lands on its wearer's shining, sharply studded, heeled black boot. Carter sips his drink and tips his head.

Another petal falls.

"This might be a silly question," Carter says, leaning to be heard over the trumpet solo. "But are you all right?"

They sit up in a sudden sweep of black hair and blink hazel eyes rimmed in smeared black eyeliner. On the bar sit two wedding bands, side by side.

Oh.

"Oh, are you—" Carter pauses; is there a non-awkward way to phrase this? "Did you… uh… get left at the altar just now?" Probably not like that.

Green-gold eyes narrow. "How did you—"

"Me too. I mean. Well. Preemptively, I suppose." Carter finishes his drink and shakes it above his head to get the attention of the bartender. Of course, someone else was dumped today; Matthew's long-lost love certainly wasn't marrying *herself*. Yet, in his noble sacrifice for true love, he'd not considered that someone else's heart would be broken today. There isn't much he can do about it now, though he feels obligated to reach out all the same. "Mint julep?"

Three drinks later, Carter is bobbing his head to the music. His new neighbor in Dumpedville, propped up on the bar by one arm, is twisted around to scrutinize him. "Aren't you miserable?"

Carter taps his feet. "Probably." His shakes his head and knocks back another swig. "See, the key is, you have to take your feelings, gather them up, and then *crush* them." He demonstrates said crushing with his free hand.

"That's a tad cynical," his new friend says. "Don't you think?"

Carter takes a gulp of yet another fresh drink, wincing a little at the burn in his throat. "I find that a healthy dose of cynicism prepares me for the inevitable disappointments in life." Carter hums, raising his glass as if in a toast. "Life is but a series of closed doors and people slamming them in your face." He says this cheerily, slurring a little, to his new companion's arched eyebrow.

"You know, you may be onto something. What was your name again?"

Had he said? He's started to lose track of things. "Carter. Carter Jacob."

"Your name is backward," his new pal in misery says.

Carter laughs. It is, isn't it? That is *hilarious*. Carter orders another drink for himself. "And—they? Will have another one also." Carter turns, eyebrows raised. He tries to not assume.

"Actually, if you could stick with they…"

"Sure," Carter says. "Easy-peasy." Oh, he's more than buzzed; he never says "easy-peasy." After taking another drink to shore up his confidence, Carter says, "I'm bi. And my family cannot seem to take that at face value. They can't *understand* it." Carter's drink sloshes with his angry gesticulations. "But I'm not asking them to understand it. I'm asking them to accept that I know who I am, more than they do. Simple as that. So. You know."

"I'm Link, by the way."

Link's face is bemused, Carter thinks, or just confused. It's a nice face either way, quite lovely, with a wide, full-lipped mouth, slanted cheekbones, and a sharp jaw. Standing upright, they're long-limbed and graceful. Their green-gold eyes dart over Carter. Carter tries out the name of his new best friend in his sluggish, slow mouth. "A pleasure to make your acquaintance, Link," he says, which Link finds quite funny, probably because Carter spends some time stumbling over the word "acquaintance." Carter's mouth stretches into a grin. He should have little to smile about—and yet.

Link shrugs off their tuxedo coat to reveal a ruffled dress shirt like those shirts in '70s prom photos; it's hideous, but on Link it works. The oversized, lime-green collar falls open across curved collarbones and a swath of smooth skin. The band takes five, and Carter forces his lingering gaze away from Link's neck and clavicles. Without the music, Carter becomes newly aware of the emptiness of the little bar space; just he and Link and the bartender are here now.

"I sent everyone away," Link says to Carter's scan of the empty tables. "Couldn't take them all looking at me. It was humiliating enough." Link gestures with their glass to the vacant, reception-less courtyard. "Needed to wallow in peace, you know."

Carter remembers that he has no room to stay in, no plans for how or when he's getting back to Illinois, and here he's barnacled himself to Link instead of getting on and dealing with it. "I can…" He jerks his head toward the exit.

"No, stay. It's nice have someone in the same boat." Link scrunches up their face. "Not that I'm *glad* you're suffering the same fate. Not exactly."

Carter nods his head a few too many times; his brain is wobbly. "No, yeah. No, I get it." They both look around the quiet, solemn room where Link should have been celebrating a new marriage. Instead, here are the two of them: the collateral damage, the miscellaneous leftovers. The thought is sobering, and it's time for something stronger, anywhere else.

"Do you want to get out of here?" Link says. Carter is already sliding off his stool. Outside, tuxedo jacket balled beneath one arm and skirt ruffling gently in the mildly cold breeze, Link summons an Uber. Carter can't make the ground stay steady, goes stumbling backward, and slumps against a wall to get his bearings. He admires the recessed arched windows and doors of the hotel's exterior; the shutters appear to be the original batten made of heavy mahogany to keep out the harsh sun and extreme weather of the swampy, hurricane-prone, deep South. It's classic New Orleans: simple, sturdy, and elegant all in the same package. A car pulls up to the curb, and Link calls out.

Carter trails his fingers along the intricate pattern of the wrought iron gate. "Ooh, filigree," he says, joining Link. "Nice."

The flower pinned to Link's jacket has completely lost its petals. "Carter Jacob," Link says, steadying Carter as he stumbles into the car, "are you this cute all the time?"

Carter frowns. Did Matthew ever think he was cute? "I don't know," Carter answers. Right now, he's no longer sure of anything.

CARTER OPENS HIS EYES TO a strange hotel room. The sound of knocking on the door reverberates painfully through his skull. His entire body throbs. The sun blasts cruelly from behind a lace curtain. Carter closes his eyes. He sits up slowly when the knocking starts again. He is wearing someone else's clothes: a black T-shirt and teeny-tiny shorts. Someone else is sleeping next to him. He has no idea how he got here.

Link.

Link's hair is done up in a French braid. Carter has no recollection of that happening. He twists out of the covers, groans, stands slowly, and presses a hand against the wall. The room spins, and sickly heat crawls up Carter's spine. He recalls a different bar; there were shots. And then, somehow, they were here. He opens the door.

"Sorry to wake you, Mr. Kline."

Carter tries to say *who?* or *what?* but it comes out as a mumbled, "Whnuf?"

The concierge's eyes slip to Carter's too-tight borrowed T-shirt; it's no doubt perfectly snug on Link's long body, but on Carter it bunches unattractively. He struggles to tug it straight, getting a glimpse of the bold white lettering on its front: QUEER AS IN FUCK U. The concierge's eyes widen, and their cheeks redden.

Carter clears his throat.

"Ah. Yes. An en suite breakfast is part of your honeymoon package, if you remember." The concierge gestures to a cart loaded with covered trays of food. Carter's stomach growls, then lurches. He quickly presses a hand over his mouth; he's too confused and hungover to stop the concierge from pushing the cart inside, then handing Carter a receipt. "If you could just sign at the bottom."

The food has been pre-charged to the room; the card belongs to Jamie Kline. Jamie… Matthew's Jamie… Link's former Jamie…

The events of yesterday slot back into place. Carter's stomach sours even further. He wants to crawl under the covers and slip back into blissfully ignorant unconsciousness, but the concierge stands there with an expectant look on their face for a long, uncomfortable moment until Carter realizes that he's supposed to offer a tip.

"Right." Carter searches for his pants, where he hopes his wallet is still tucked into the front right pocket. Clothes and bedding are strewn everywhere; an empty champagne bottle sits in the center of the room. It looks exactly as though he and Link had a very celebratory, very naked honeymoon night. Carter is not entirely sure they didn't.

He locates his pants, draped over a floor lamp, and his wallet. Also tucked into his pockets are hints of what happened the night before: a cocktail napkin from a bar, a pot of glittery something, a tarot card, and a matchbook from a place called "Ye Olde Absinthe House."

No wonder he can't remember anything.

Carter tips the concierge, then stumbles into the bathroom to splash cold water on his face. In the mirror, his skin is glittery and strange. Gold eyeshadow is painted over his eyes and across his cheeks; blotches of pink linger at the corners of his lips. His fingernails are painted pink. Carter has a sudden flash of sitting at a bar and having a very earnest conversation about the depressing restrictions of the gender binary. Then he and Link decided to get makeovers, he remembers, but isn't sure if that was before or after the absinthe bar. Carter rubs at his throbbing head and turns on the shower. Under the stream of hot water, the nausea and thumping headache ease. As he washes off the night before with the plain bar of hotel soap, glitter twirls festively down the drain. He wanted the quintessential New Orleans experience and he got it. Unfortunately, he does not remember much of it.

Carter is wrapping a fluffy white towel around his waist when the door bangs open and Link stumbles into the steamy bathroom with both hands pressed over their mouth, then stops with wide, shocked eyes to take in Carter's bare torso and only partly covered groin. Carter squeaks and flaps the towel closed. Link hunches over the toilet.

He's had some less-than-enthusiastic intimate partners over the years, but this is a first.

"Sorry," Link says later, sweet-smelling and still damp from a shower.

"No, it's…" He trails off, because nothing is okay in the unflinching bright light of day. "Um. Thanks for letting me crash here." Carter is fully dressed now, in his clothes from yesterday that smell like a frat house plus absinthe and nail polish. He'll need to change before getting on a plane to go home.

"Yeah. No problem." Link attempts a pleasant smile, but winces instead. They're so much softer this morning in wide, loose pants and a snug cotton T-shirt, hair tied back and barefoot, curled up against the headboard of the king-sized bed. "Are you hungry? I don't think I can eat." Link gestures at the food cart.

Carter *is* a little hungry, despite the clench of nausea still holding fast. He hasn't had anything solid in his stomach since lunch at the airport in Chicago. Matthew was being so strange then, so irritable and distant. No wonder. Carter picks up the trays of food that Link and his fiancée probably picked out together for their first morning as a married couple. Sadness creeps into the room like heavy fog. Carter nibbles on dry toast and searches for flights while his phone charges with Link's charging cord.

"Do you mind if I have them bring up my suitcase so I can change before I go?"

Link stares blankly at a wall and makes a brief noise of agreement.

There's quick rap on the door almost immediately after Carter hangs up. "Wow, that was fast. Impressive." It's too bad Matthew didn't actually book them a room; he'd love to stay longer. It's a very nice, beautifully historic hotel, but he also really, really doesn't want to go home and face everyone yet.

The concierge doesn't hand him his suitcase, however, but a picnic basket and checkered blanket. Blinking in bafflement, Carter takes them. There has been some serious miscommunication with the front desk. "Uhhh," he says.

"Your chariot awaits." The concierge bows.

"Er," Carter replies.

"The horse-drawn carriage ride and picnic at City Park," Link says in a flat voice from the bed, their face etched with sadness. Link will have to face this chipper concierge and tell them that the wedding is off, the marriage is off. That it's just Link, all alone and left behind, just as Carter is. And Carter can't allow that. He can't stand to see Link so sad and lifeless, to stand by and let them relive that humiliation and heartbreak. He can't remember exactly what happened last night, but he feels bonded to Link, protective of Link's broken heart as if it's now connected permanently with his own. What happened to both of them is not right, and it's not fair.

"Of course! Our romantic carriage ride. That we planned. The two of us. Together. Yes, thank you! We'll be right down!" Carter slams the door closed.

Link stares at him, unblinking. Carter shifts awkwardly with the picnic basket and blanket piled in his arms. Maybe he was completely out of line. Maybe Link wishes Carter would go away and leave them alone. Maybe Carter's suggestion that he would go on a romantic horse-drawn carriage ride intended for someone else's honeymoon was the worst choice he's made on this trip. Then Link's lovely mouth curves into a soft, sweet smile.

"Thank you. You totally saved me."

Carter's head dips; his heart flutters strangely. Maybe, just a little bit, in this awful and strange situation, they've saved each other.

THREE

"So how long were you two together?" Link is stretched out on one side, a hand propping up their head, the other tracing the gingham pattern of the picnic blanket. The picnic is spread beneath a massive, old-growth oak tree, and a grassy green field stretches all around, stopping where a lake ripples gray and placid against the blue skyline.

"Seven years," Carter says, spreading brie on a thin slice of baguette. He's leaning against the huge trunk of the tree between two gnarled and knotted roots that rise from the ground beside him like armrests.

"Wow," Link says. They've been nibbling on chocolate-covered strawberries, and a collection of green stems are scattered around the blanket. "That's a long time."

Carter chews and nods. "You know, when he proposed, we laughed and said something about it being 'about that time.' Which may have been a red flag, looking back on it."

Link reaches for another strawberry. "Jamie and I were only together for eight months. *We* were hell-bent on fast-tracking everything, and I never stopped to think about why that might be." After nibbling one more strawberry, Link lifts their glass of sparkling water—they'd both decided it was best to forgo the champagne today—and toasts, "Here's to ignoring red flags!"

Carter leans forward to tip his glass against Link's. Wind chimes of all sizes and types are strung throughout the branches, and, when the wind is strong enough, it stirs a lilting, soft melody that matches the undulation of the water nearby. In any other circumstance, it would have made for a very romantic picnic, but for Carter and Link it's a soundtrack of melancholy as they discuss their exes and how everything went so wrong. Could he have stopped it? Should he have? Spared Link, if not himself?

"We should talk about something else," Carter says, opening a container of gourmet French pastries. Link scoots a little closer and takes a cream-filled mille-feuille.

"Okay. What do you do back in Aurora, Illinois, Carter Jacob?"

Carter smiles; he likes the way Link says his name. "I'm an architect."

"Wait. That's a real thing that people do?" Link says with a teasing grin.

"Yes. It is a real thing." Carter pulls the container of pastries out of Link's reach as payback for the ribbing. "I work for a big company that designs large suburban houses. And actually, I'm a production architect, which means…" He trails off. This is usually the part when his conversation partner's eyes glaze over. "It's boring. Never mind."

Link gazes up, eyes challenging. "Do you think it's boring?"

"No." Why does Link make him feel compelled to share his emotional truths? He doesn't even like to tell himself his true feelings. "I don't find it boring. I mean it is, because I mostly deal with practicalities and inputting data, double-checking building codes and measurements, and emailing back and forth with contractors. Someone has to take everyone's wild dreams and make them a reality." Carter pokes at the cream escaping one end of an éclair, licks it off his fingertip, and says, "Practicality isn't exactly sexy."

Link glances from the éclair, to Carter's mouth, then back to hold Carter's eyes. "No?"

Carter struggles to swallow the bit of cream. His voice is too high when he asks, "So. What, uh, what do you do?"

"I'm an artist, mostly sculptures welded from recycled scrap metal," Link says. "Statues and furniture and stuff."

Carter lifts his eyebrows. "And *that's* a real thing?"

Link's responding laugh mixes with the sound of the wind chimes. Flopping over onto their back, Link's tight T-shirt rides up, revealing the smooth curves of their stomach and soft-looking skin. Carter lies back beside them, his body stretched out opposite, with his head at Link's purple-sneakered feet, resting side by side. He picks a matching purple wildflower near his shoulder and cheekily puts it into Link's inverted belly button. The sun has mellowed, and the shadow of the oak tree is pleasantly chilly. The wind chimes and rustling leaves and lapping of the lake create a lazy, hypnotic melody.

"This is kind of nice," Link murmurs, and Carter repeats it in agreement. He could fall asleep and stay here forever. He can't, of course.

"I am not looking forward to going home and facing everyone," Carter says with a sigh. He has no idea who knows and how much they know. Matthew was the social media junkie, not Carter, so he never bothered to keep anyone in the loop on his own. And, for all Carter knows, he's now the talk of Twitter or whatever.

"Ugh, me either," Link groans. "You have no idea how much artists like to gossip."

Carter takes a moment to imagine that and then imagines the "I told you so" lecture he'll get from his sister. She never liked Matthew and she loves being right even more than she loves gossip. "Hey, by the way." Carter tips his head to the side and squints at Link close-up. "Did we hook up last night?"

Link's relaxed expression doesn't budge. "Nah."

"Oh," Carter says, unsure of how he feels about that. "Do you remember?"

"No, but my chastity belt is still securely locked," Link says, deadpan. "Yes, I remember."

Carter looks back up at the tree. "Okay. That's... good."

"Oh, really? Not disappointed you missed out on all of this, hmm?" From the corner of his eye, Carter can see Link gesture to their body and face. "That hurts, Carter Jacob."

It's not that Carter doesn't find Link attractive; he finds a wide variety of people attractive, generally, and Link specifically. "I just prefer to remember sleeping with someone is all." Carter blinks and reconsiders that statement. "Well, I guess I wouldn't mind forgetting some of them."

Matthew, for a start. "Do you remember anything else?" Carter asks, changing the subject. Best not to dwell too long on any attraction he has to Link; it's not appropriate for the situation, and he'll be gone soon anyway.

"Let's see…" Link hums. "We went to a fortune teller." *That explains the tarot card.* "And," Link continues, "karaoke?"

"Damn. I'd prided myself on never singing drunken karaoke." He is really checking off a bucket list he never wanted to make.

Link turns to face Carter with a smirk. "Well, if it helps, I think it was less drunken karaoke and more you standing on a table randomly singing, actually."

Carter purses his lips. "That's definitely worse."

Link snorts with laughter, which makes Carter laugh despite his embarrassment. Perhaps his behavior last night was good for him, getting out of his comfort zone, doing something different and unexpected. For too long he's been stifled, ignoring the many warning signs of his own obvious unhappiness. It would have been nice if he and Matthew could have settled it quietly about eight months ago, but, as they might say in New Orleans, c'est la vie.

"Stop me if this sounds crazy," Link says, breaking Carter from his spiraling regrets, "but I have a whole week of these activities and meals bought and paid for. We get along okay; we're stuck dealing with the same crappy situation. I, for one, think we deserve daily room service after being dumped so very epically."

It's not the healthiest way of dealing with the fallout: delaying the inevitable, pretending things are fine when they aren't, and pretending to be the new husband of someone he met yesterday, someone whose fiancée has run off with *his* fiancé. Yet, when he turns to Link to say this, none of it seems to matter. Somehow, this unexpected adventure makes more sense than anything Carter has done in a long, long time. "You know what, we absolutely do. I'm in."

FOUR

As Carter waits in the line at the hotel's front desk, his phone lights up. He ignores it. He called work with a fake illness for the first time, and he's afraid someone will call him out. When he glances at the missed-call notification, he finds something much worse. The family in front of him finally finishes checking in. "A single, please. Or, whatever is available first." The clerk clacks away at the computer, and Carter hits decline on his phone a second time. He and Link are going out for the evening soon, so Carter decided to book a room first. Drunk and heartbroken Carter may be fine with crashing in the bed of a virtual stranger, but regular Carter is a little uncomfortable with it.

"All right, I have a double available on the seventeenth or a single on the eighteenth." The clerk looks up with fingers poised over the keyboard.

"Oh, uh. No, I need something tonight." Carter smiles pleasantly.

A lightning-quick look of annoyance flashes across the clerk's face before they reaffix their pleasant, helpful customer-service face. "Sir, it's two weeks before Mardi Gras. This is our most popular time. I have a double on the seventeenth or a single on the eighteenth."

Carter shakes his head and mutters, "No, thank you," as his phone rings for a third time. He steps to a quiet corner in the lobby and answers with a sigh.

"I hate to say I told you so..."

Carter rolls his eyes. "Paige, come on. No, you don't." His sister loves to be right even more than she loves Snapchat filters, which is *a lot.* "So everyone knows, then."

"Yes, and we're all wondering why you haven't come home yet," Paige says, then barrels on without giving him a chance to reply. "You know mom is thrilled. She's telling everyone that she knew you'd come to your senses."

Carter works his jaw and glares at the wallpaper. It's a green and gold fabric toile with intricate patterns of peacocks and flowers and arching vines. She has to ask why he hasn't come home yet? The better question is, why would he ever?

"Carter, you know it's just because she worries about you. Like, why make your life more difficult? If she and dad couldn't learn to like Matthew, a rich, handsome lawyer, then maybe it's worth reconsidering your choices."

Carter snaps, reflexively, "It's not a choice." It's also not news that his family considers his bisexuality to be a mere phase—one designed to wound them and, more importantly, make them look bad to their snobby, judgmental friends—but it still hurts.

Paige ignores him. "You know my friend Meredith is still single."

Her friend Meredith is twice divorced, with a shopping addiction and a penchant for collecting tiny, yappy dogs that are only slightly less obnoxious than she is. "I'm not really ready to date yet." And not interested in dating Paige's friend Meredith ever.

"Whatever, okay. Just listen, Carter. Think of this as like, a blessing. A chance to start over and get your life on track, finally. We care about you. We just want you to be happy."

Carter ends the call and rests his forehead against the wallpaper; the raised pattern is velvety soft against his skin. *We just want you to be happy.* And yet, no matter how hard he tries, no matter what he does, they never are happy with him. He never gets it right.

When Carter gets back to the room, Link is perched in front of the bathroom mirror swiping on shiny lip gloss. They've changed into skintight, white jeans that are tucked into heavy black boots and a draping, cream-colored button-down. Gold bracelets jingle on their wrists with every light, graceful movement. Gorgeous. Carter's stomach clenches, and he shifts against the closed door. He's feeling too many conflicting emotions tugging at him from all directions, sinking him.

"Are you changing? Not that you don't look cute already," Link says with a silly, flirty wink. The nausea grows in Carter's gut. "Hello? *Carter Jacob?*"

He looks at the floor. "Yeah. Uh. They didn't have any rooms."

"That's okay," Link says sweetly. "It would have been weird trying to explain to the hotel staff why my new spouse was sleeping in another room anyway." Link laughs, but Carter says nothing, just grabs a change of clothes and slinks off to the bathroom. Thank goodness he's an over-packer and planned a few nice going-out outfits. At least he won't look like a total schlub, though he feels like one.

Tonight's destination is only a few blocks away, so they walk. Carter shuffles with his hands in his pockets and shoulders high. Link swans along and chatters about various landmarks and tourist traps in the French Quarter; they're extremely knowledgeable about New Orleans. Normally Carter would be so into it, but he nods and offers a single *mhm*. His brief conversation with Paige has put a dark cloud over everything. Is Carter now so desperate not to be alone that he finds no issue with pretending to be someone's husband? Is this how he was pretending that things were fine with Matthew? What if Paige is right, and he is just making his life difficult?

The restaurant is in an old Creole-style townhouse: pink stucco on the outside and green and coral on the inside. A plaque in the waiting area says it's been there since 1942, and it looks like it, as if frozen in time and place. Link checks in at the host stand while Carter admires the intricate latticework separating sections of the restaurant, the walls made of still-sturdy, hand-shaped mud bricks, and the upstairs walkway circling the entire perimeter. "Look at that balustrade," Carter says wonderingly when Link returns. "Real marble, wow."

Link looks up with him. "The... railing?"

Carter, forgetting to be sullen and conflicted, moves next to Link and points up. "Yes, well, the railing *and* columns. Those round posts in between there are called balusters, balaustra in Italian, because they look like blossoming pomegranate flowers. The style dates from the fifteenth century and was favored by Italian royalty." Link stares up, squinting, trying to see what Carter sees. "Sorry," Carter says, "that is random and boring." Everyone hates when he does that, but he's not trying to be annoying; he just gets excited.

Link gives him a look that Carter can't read, then says, "Carter Jacob, you can info-dump about Italian architecture to me any old time." They might be teasing, Carter thinks, though Link's expression certainly appears sincere.

The host leads them upstairs and Carter *has to* talk about the Norman truss on the pitched ceiling and the difference between a king post truss and a Norman truss while a waiter takes drink orders.

Link explains their work in more detail: the process of salvaging and piecing together old metal gears and chains and bicycle and engine parts to create something new from something old. Carter is fascinated, transfixed by the excitement in Link's eyes, the way their full lips form around the words, the quick, expressive movement of their hands as Link explains welding a recent sculpture. It seems like no time all before their entrées arrive: seafood gumbo for Carter and Link's Creole-spiced shrimp salad.

"You know, I'm Creole on my mom's side," Link says. "Part Cajun on my paternal side."

"No kidding? That's fascinating." Everything about Link is fascinating. A tealight flickers on the table between them, and all the lovely contours of Link's face take on a dramatic, sharp glow. "So you have roots here, then?"

Link chews and nods. "I do. Then all over, doing the nomadic, freewheeling-artist thing for a while. And lately, I've really wanted to settle down. Have a home. Someone to come home to. I guess part of why—" They wave their fork, indicating the two of them, clearly meaning the post-dumped situation they've found themselves in. "I wanted it too badly."

"Well, perhaps I didn't want it badly enough," Carter confesses. For so long he thought it was him, that maybe he didn't stir strong romantic feelings in anyone, that perhaps love always felt like settling and that was okay. He now knows that isn't true. It was just that Matthew had real, true feelings for someone else.

Link flicks a hand to dismiss the sad route they're heading down. "Anyway. How did you end up in Aurora?"

"Born and raised," Carter says. He scoops up gumbo; it is delicious. "I always thought I would leave and then I... didn't." He never found a compelling enough reason to go elsewhere, though he was still in Aurora only incidentally.

"Well, you have family and friends there, right?" Link says diplomatically. "A good job. Stability. That's important."

Carter moves his gumbo around the bowl and doesn't answer; his mood shifts again. Carter wishes Link wasn't so nice to him. The more time the two of them spend together, the more Carter is drawn to Link, and the more he knows he can't be. In six days, Carter is going home to a place he doesn't want to be, to a life he built around someone who left him and a family who will never accept him. There are worse things, certainly. But there are better ones, too, and he can only pretend otherwise for so long.

FIVE

THE HOTEL ROOM SEEMS TO have become smaller as Carter and Link maneuver around each other while getting ready for bed. There's no way to not brush up against Link as they sort through a huge suitcase in the tiny hallway by the bathroom, no way to undress without being overly aware of the single thin door separating him from Link and how much of him Link has already seen. Carter emerges from the bathroom in the thin satin pajamas he bought for special occasions.

Link whistles. "Fancy."

Carter ducks his head and wishes he'd brought sweatpants. "I, uh, was under the impression that this trip was going to be something different, so…"

"Yeah," Link says, their tone suddenly bitter. This was supposed to be a honeymoon. "Guess I won't be wearing my sexy lingerie." Carter can't tell if they're joking. He can't tell if he wants them to be. At Carter's awkward silence, Link nods toward the bathroom. "I'm just gonna…"

They dance around each other so Link can pass, both of them moving right, then left, then right together. Link chuckles at the clichéd predicament and grasps Carter's elbow to keep him still as they stand a breath apart. Heat spikes along Carter's skin. He lunges away from Link's touch and clambers onto the bed to remove himself from the way-too-close proximity. While Link is in the bathroom, Carter takes three steadying breaths, then searches for extra linens in the large antique bureau, and finds only a single sad, coarse blanket.

I'm just lonely, Carter reminds himself. The two of them get along, sure; they have an easy camaraderie, yes; Link is attractive, definitely; but doing anything under the circumstances… It's a bad idea.

He's situating the thin brown blanket on the floor between the bed and the wall when Link comes out of the bathroom, not in lingerie, but in cotton shorts and a T-shirt. Carter drops a pillow on top of the blanket and tries to convince himself that the tight space will be cozy and not claustrophobic.

"Are you gonna fit?" Link asks, perching on the far side of the bed.

Carter tips his head. "Yes?" On his side, he should, probably. Mostly.

"You could just—" Link gestures at the other side of the bed. "I don't want to make you uncomfortable or anything…"

"I was trying to not make *you* uncomfortable."

Link sighs, gathering up their hair up into a messy twist. "This is dumb. We already shared the bed once—"

"Drunk," Carter points out.

"Yes, drunk, but still." Link's hands drop and their hair tumbles loose to their shoulders. "We're adults. I think we can handle sharing a bed without accidentally dry-humping each other in the middle of the night."

Carter considers this with his jaw set. That blanket does look very uncomfortable. "All right," he concedes. It is a pretty large bed. Carter perches on the edge. "Do adults really call it 'dry-humping,' though?"

Link seems embarrassed until Carter smiles, then laughs and pushes at Carter's shoulder. "Yes, we do." After turning off the lamp next to their side of the bed, Link curls under the covers. Carter does the same, and quiet settles into the room, until Link says in the dark, "What would you call it?"

Flipping to his back, on the very far side of his side of the bed, Carter says, "I don't know. Foreplay?"

Link hums. "Fair enough."

In the quiet darkness, it's impossible for Carter to keep his mind from drifting to Matthew and his own family and the unhappy life waiting for him back in Aurora, then to all the missteps that led him here, and how he's coping with the fallout by not coping with it and dragging Link down with him. Maybe he should just go home.

"Hey, Carter?" Link says, voice soft with sleep.

"Yeah?"

"Thank you. For staying with me. It's… helping."

"Sure," Carter says. He is anything but sure.

Carter wakes abruptly from a fragmented dream of cascading coins and racing chariots and chasing something perpetually out of reach. The room is gray with watery pre-dawn light, and Carter's only coherent thought is irritation that he woke before his alarm sounded. Closing his eyes, determined to sleep a little longer before he has to trudge off to work, Carter tugs the blanket tighter around his shoulders. He always runs extra cold on winter nights, stacks blankets and seeks out the body heat of the person next to him in bed, flinging an arm over, tucking legs between, pushing his pelvis against a hip, unthinkingly grinding against the early-morning ache between his legs.

Carter realizes too late that this morning the person in bed next to him is not Matthew.

Carter flings himself back, startling Link from sleep. "Sorry. Sorry, sorry."

"'S'okay," Link mumbles, then rolls over and goes right back to sleep.

Carter is wide awake, awake and aroused and embarrassed. Several deep breaths have no effect on his situation, so Carter gives up on sleeping and scurries off for a cold shower.

"Aren't you an early bird this morning?" An hour or so later, Link finds Carter on the balcony, where he's wrapped up in the terrible brown blanket. Link hands over a cup of coffee, sits close, but not too close, on the little bench, and tugs a corner of the blanket over their lap. "I conked out last night. Don't remember a *thing*." Link is saying it for his benefit, graciously letting him off the hook. It doesn't make Carter feel any less awkward. Apparently, he *can't* sleep next to Link without dry-humping them. He should have slept on the floor.

Propping one foot on the wrought iron gabling, Carter sips his coffee, says nothing, and watches the morning sun cast the whole city block in a golden glow. There's nothing else to say, nothing to be done about it now; he's apologized and he can add it to the list of things he's pretending are fine and normal.

Together he and Link watch the city below come to vibrant, busy life with the streets and sidewalks full of people passing by, going in and out of shops and restaurants. A carriage like the one they took to their picnic yesterday bumps by, pulled by two white horses trotting at a steady pace. One busker plays harmonica on a corner, another dances to a song playing from a boombox; a street artist spray-paints colorful galaxies next to a vendor selling street-food delicacies. In New Orleans, Carter could be someone else living a different life, one full of color and sound and light.

"I love it here," Carter says to himself.

"Nothing like it," Link agrees. "Ooh! You know what you need to have? Beignets at Café du Monde. It's not just for tourists; locals actually eat there too."

"Sure, yeah," Carter agrees.

Link glances at him over the top of their steaming coffee cup. "Are we okay?"

We. Carter frowns. There is no such thing. There can't be. The fantasy life he imagined for himself is just that. A fantasy. "Sure." Carter says, then changes the subject. "So, beignets?"

SIX

CARTER DOESN'T KNOW LINK VERY well at all, and yet the cemetery tour on the honeymoon itinerary for today is exactly the sort of thing Carter expects Link to be interested in. It is not something Carter would ever choose, but he's happy enough to go along, as Link's bubbly happiness when they arrive at the tour headquarters makes Carter fizzle with something like excitement too.

On the tour bus, Link is downright giddy, bouncing in the seat next to Carter as the tour guide explains the history of Saint Louis Cemetery No. 1: It is the oldest cemetery in New Orleans, famous for its above-ground crypts. As they file off the bus, the guide says that Mark Twain once dubbed these cemeteries "Cities of the Dead," and for good reason: the tombs could be small houses, laid out in an architecturally gothic neighborhood of final resting places.

"Nicolas Cage has a plot here," Link says, breaking off from the group and turning down a narrow passageway between crumbling brick and stucco tombs as if they know exactly where to go.

Carter frowns. "Nicolas Cage is dead?"

"Nope," Link moves quickly along the path; their long gray scarf flutters behind them like a ghost.

Though well within the city and with busy freeways sprawling nearby, the cemetery is hushed; just the crunch of footsteps and the quiet howl of the wind twisting through the grave sites keep them company. Together, Carter and Link pause to read the inscriptions, the ones that aren't worn down by age and weather, then continue in silence. At a tomb of a husband and wife, buried together, Carter stops as Link moves on. *Together for eternity.* Is that Carter wants? Is it what

Matthew was looking for and found with someone else? If Jamie was the one who got away, then what the hell does that make Carter? He'd committed to Matthew. He had planned a forever with Matthew. And now he has no plans, no future to look toward, no one who is interested in sharing a life with him, let alone an eternal afterlife.

"Oh, Jacqueline and Louis," Carter says to the double marble tomb, to the people who have been dead for two hundred years. "You have no idea how lucky you are."

"Carter!" Link's voice comes from a few rows down. When Carter finally finds where they are, the rest of the tour group is already milling nearby. "Check it out."

"*Barthélemy Lafon,*" Carter reads. He turns to Link for further explanation.

"Notable architect and pirate. That's one way to inject a little excitement in your career." Link makes a pirate-like *arrr* noise and laughs. It's hard to feel anything but joy when Link laughs like that.

"I don't know," Carter says, flat and serious. "I get pretty bad seasickness."

There's a moment when Link seems to be trying to figure out if Carter's serious. Then they laugh again. "But otherwise…"

"Otherwise I'd for sure be an architect-pirate," Carter says, in the same serious tone. Link bumps against him, still smiling, then stays pressed close as the tour moves on.

"Known as the Voodoo Queen, Marie Laveau's life remains shrouded in mystery," the tour guide says, rounding a corner with the rest of the group. "After her internment here in 1881, she was said to be spotted walking around the French Quarter the *very next day.*" He pauses for dramatic effect, then claps his hands. "And that's all for the guided tour folks, feel free to look around until we board the bus for our next stop on the Haunted New Orleans Tour. And by the way," he says as the group starts to wander in all directions, "we have newlyweds on our tour today!"

Back turned to the tour group and Link, Carter's stomach drops.

"Congratulations to Link and Jamie!"

Carter turns to find Link wide-eyed and frozen in place as the tour guide and group all turn their attention directly to Link. Carter moves without thinking, taking Link's hand in his and holding it high as if taking a victory lap.

"Thanks, everyone!" Carter says. Everyone claps. Carter keeps Link's hand tight in his even while everyone gathers to move on, no longer paying the two of them any attention.

"Are we selling this?" Carter whispers while waiting to board the bus.

"I think so..." Link's hand in his is warm and soft. The rings on their fingers shift, cool against Carter's skin; bracelets flutter and drag along the inside of Carter's wrist. The line to board the bus moves forward, and Carter's knuckles brush the jut of Link's hip.

"Are my hands sweaty?" Despite the February chill, Carter is hot all over.

Link's hand shifts, thumb stroking shivery down Carter's palm. "No, you're good."

On the bus to the next stop, he and Link sit a little closer, as a newly-wed couple might. Carter has to strip to his shirt, roll up the sleeves, and open the window.

He's good. Good, good. Good.

The tour takes them to a haunted pharmacy and a haunted jazz club, a haunted cathedral and a haunted morgue, which seems a little on the nose to Carter. He and Link follow along dutifully, hand in hand and arm in arm, so committed to their happily, newly married ruse that, when Link drapes an arm around Carter's waist as they enter the last stop—a haunted bar—it feels normal, almost. Very nearly real. Carter slips his arm around Link's back.

Everything is lit with dripping wax candles; there is no electricity at all in the old blacksmith-shop-turned-bar. Someone buys drinks for the newlyweds, and everyone toasts the happy couple. The drink is purple and slushy and sickly sweet, making Carter's teeth ache with every sip. Link is holding court with a circle of people, saying something

French, or sort of French, laughing and gesturing emphatically, so full of life, so beautiful.

Carter can't look away.

Link is not Carter's anything; he shouldn't be looking at them the way he is, and yet he and Link are caught here together in this temporary in-between space, this real and not-real which is as much a purgatory as the spaces inhabited by nonexistent ghosts on this haunted tour. So, as long as they're pretending anyway... He slips his arm tighter around Link's sharp-boned hips, tugging them closer.

"This drink tastes like the bastard child of Captain Morgan and the Kool-Aid Man," Link says, and Carter throws his head back in laughter. It really does.

"You guys seems so happy," comments a familiar face from the tour; at the cemetery, they'd made rubbings of names and dates with crayon and paper. "How did you meet?"

Carter opens his mouth and says nothing; he looks at Link, who stutters nonsense. Then Carter answers, "The bank," just as Link supplies a response of, "An orgy." Carter's eyes widen, and he has to look away from Link, who is red-faced and seconds from bursting into laughter.

Carter considers offering further explanation—an orgy for bankers? An orgy at a bank?—but anything he can come up with will make things worse, and anyway, Link's shoulders are trembling with barely contained laughter. Carter, pretending to be suddenly distracted, sets down his terrible drink and pulls out his phone. He holds it up in explanation. "Excuse us."

A staircase looms in a dark corner of the bar; a heavy hemp rope blocks it off and folding chairs are stacked against it. Here the noise of the bar fades just enough to let them talk in low voices. "Sorry," Link says, laughing, not looking sorry at all. "That popped into my brain for some reason."

Carter has to ask, "Who are you meeting at orgies?"

"Who are you meeting at banks?" Link replies.

He met Matthew through a friend of a friend who thought they would be compatible, possibly an even more boring scenario than meeting at a bank. Carter waves off the question. "I think everyone is on to us now." He glances at the crowd. A few people seem to be looking for them, perhaps even discussing them as obvious fakes.

"Good thing we never have to see anybody here ever again, then." Link takes a long sip of the frozen purple drink through the festive twisty straw, then shudders and sets it on a stair. "Unless we're all now connected in the afterlife! Maybe *we'll* be the ghosts of the old blacksmith shop."

Even in this creepy, dark corner of a creepy, dark bar there is nothing remotely haunting going on besides the lingering taste of that disgusting drink. "There is no ghost of the blacksmith shop," Carter says, impatiently.

"Says you," Link retorts.

Carter rolls his eyes. "An entire day spent in haunted places and *nothing*. I want a refund. There should be a money-back no-hauntings clause if one is claiming to offer a haunted tour."

"A skeptic." Link's arms cross, and they lean forward into Carter's space; Carter mimics them, tilting his head so they're nearly nose to nose. Carter's eyes slip to Link's teasing mouth before he can stop himself. He snaps his gaze away as Link begins to speak. "The legend of the old blacksmith shop is that the blacksmith himself haunts the downstairs area. And upstairs…" Link flicks their head toward the pitch blackness at the top of the staircase. "Is where the spirit of a woman scorned roams the halls."

"Oh, come on," Carter says. "They're not even trying with that one. So obvious."

Link dares him to go up and see if he's so sure, and he is, so Carter hikes one leg over the heavy, fraying rope while Link checks to see if anyone is watching, then scurries up the stairs behind Carter. Each step groans louder than the last, probably on purpose for a faux-spooky effect. Upstairs is dark, impossibly so; no candlelight reaches the space, no windows let in halos of streetlights or the soft glow of the moon. Carter blinks and blinks until his eyes adjust enough to make out three open doorways surrounding a short hallway. They're like bedrooms, but it's impossible to see what's inside.

Behind him, Link whispers, low and ominous in Carter's ear, "She would wait for him up here. Night after night after night. He never came back for her. Still, she waits. *For eternity.*"

Carter turns his head to tell Link how ridiculous that is, and that the idea of ghosts only exists because people see what they want to see, and further, why would she wait an eternity? The very notion—

One of the doors slams closed. Carter jumps and yelps and clutches Link in terror.

"Uh," Carter says, his face now very, very close to Link's face, his arms now wrapped very tightly around Link's body.

Link lifts one eyebrow, glances at Carter's lips, and says, "Boo."

SEVEN

"I HATE YOU."

"Oh, pshh." Link twirls a french fry. "It was hilarious, and you know it."

The diner where they've ended up, where harsh white lights glint on harshly shining floors, seems to exist in direct contrast to the dim bar. The chrome tables and counter and kitchen gleam bright silver, the walls blush pink, the chairs clash garish red. Over chili fries and a ham and cheese omelet, Carter and Link blame each other for the ghostly encounter.

"You slammed the door, Link. I know it."

"You angered the spirit with your disbelief!"

Top 40 hits whine from a brightly lit jukebox; a cook dances and sings along. Across from him, Link hums, scarf unwound from their graceful neck, hair now gathered into a messy bun, shoulders moving in time to a Black Eyed Peas song.

"Do you believe in that stuff? Ghosts?" Carter stabs a square of ham onto his fork.

Link chews, head tipping side to side. "I guess I believe in the possibility of there being something else—somewhere else, after we're gone from here. Something that maybe we don't fully understand." Carter nods. He can get on board with that, until Link continues, "But I *do* believe in Sasquatch."

Carter rolls his eyes and laughs at the joke. Carter hopes it's a joke, anyway. The diner, at nearly midnight, has attracted a fascinating mixed crowd of still-drunk college kids, paramedics between shifts, an elderly couple that seem to be as permanent a fixture as the grease stains on the ceiling, a handful of drag queens, and one burly guy in a trucker hat. The jukebox switches from "I Gotta Feeling" to "Bye Bye Bye" to "Bette Davis Eyes." Between bites of chili fries, Link stacks coffee creamer cups in a wobbling tower and hums along to every song.

"You need a solid base," Carter points out, fork waving over the stack of creamers. "Can't build something stable from something unstable."

Carefully setting one more creamer cup on their leaning tower, Link glances up at Carter with a smirk. "I see you trying to prove your job is real, Carter Jacob."

"It is real," Carter says. "Unlike ghosts or Sasquatch." He starts on his own tower to prove his point, creating a solid ringed base to build up from. "I'll show you."

"Ooh, it's on!" Links wiggles in the seat. "You forget I'm an artist who works in a variety of building mediums. Do not underestimate me."

"I wouldn't dare." Carter looks up, catching Link's eyes in a brief, charged moment.

The competition takes off from there, and Carter, in his haste to catch up to Link's tower, accidentally knocks his over twice and declares that doesn't count because he hadn't finished. Link cheats, too, snatching even more creamer cups from the three tables nearby, then sits smugly behind a towering and unstable completed stack. They've finished first, but one bump to the table and the whole thing will topple. As Carter finishes his much more careful and much less ostentatious design, Link tells him about a bed frame they created from nothing but old gears and a bench from only washers and tiny bolts.

It's impressive, and Carter is envious of Link's creative freedom, but when Link reaches for their drink, slightly jostling the table in the process, the whole tower tumbles.

"See? Creativity needs to be grounded in something first," Carter gloats, even giving the table a shake to prove how solid his creamer cup dome is.

"Pshh," Link says, leaning back against the booth, twirling a finger through one loose tendril of hair while smiling and sizing Carter up.

"So, Carter Jacob, building master. What is your ideal home, then? Since you spend so much time designing them for other people. A dome?"

Carter scoffs. "No, of course not. That was just the shape that suited the building materials. I don't know if I—" He stops short. He *does* have an ideal home in mind, but it was never one he could get Matthew on board for, so he'd let it go: a pipe dream, impractical. Until this very moment, he'd not considered that he no longer needs Matthew to get on board with anything at all. "I have always thought about fixing up an older home. Something with really good bones that I can put my mark on. Take my time. Not like those shoddy house flippers just looking to make a quick buck. Like a high-quality restoration."

"You should do it then," Link says, as if it's that easy.

"I don't think so," Carter stabs his straw around the ice in his cup. Just because he can now doesn't mean he should. "It's a huge undertaking. With a pretty demanding full-time job and an—" He almost says *an upcoming wedding* because, for a second, he forgot. "Uh. Not enough time. It's isn't practical."

"Okay, that makes sense." Link leans forward and plucks pink packets of Sweet 'N Low from the dispenser on the table, then sets them carefully in a pattern across the top of Carter's coffee creamer dome. It looks almost like a flower. "Being grounded and practical is important; I'll give you that. Sometimes, though, you need a little flair."

Back in the hotel room in the wee hours of the morning, Carter stacks pillows in a makeshift sea wall between his side and Link's side of the bed. He's never had an issue with accidental nocturnal humping, but once is enough to make him cautious. Like the night before, once he's in bed and trying to sleep with nothing else to occupy his mind, Carter's thoughts drift to Matthew. He doesn't know how to untwine his life from someone he was with for seven years. His home, his friends, his meals, his plans, his bed, all shared. Back in Aurora, Carter doesn't even know who he is without Matthew. Soon his sleepy thoughts of Matthew turn to wisps, to mist, then re-form in the shape of Link.

Here with Link, somehow, Carter feels parts of himself coming back, notices an ease in his own skin he hasn't felt in a while. He can talk to Link freely about his interests and himself without worrying that he's being weird or annoying or rambling on too long. The dreams he'd put away for Matthew now seem possible again: fixing up an old house, living somewhere else, pushing himself out of his comfort zone, trying new things in a new place, the way he always thought he would. Carter needed Matthew to love him, but deep down he knew that Matthew didn't love all of him. Link seems to like all of him.

"Carter?" Link's voice probes across the dark. "You still awake?"

Carter shifts, gathering his thoughts and tucking them away. A pillow blocks his view. "Yes, I'm awake."

"I just wanted to say—" The bed dips, the covers swish. "Is it crazy to say that this feels real sometimes? Like I forget we aren't—sometimes."

Carter stares at the pillow, thinks of moving it away so he can look into Link's eyes, so he can scoot closer, so he can touch them. "I don't think it's crazy. I think..." He thinks he and Link have this connection that is now beyond being castoffs in Jamie and Matthew's story, and that Carter is obviously drawn to Link. But he also thinks that they're both still too vulnerable for him to act on it, even if Link feels the same. *If.* Carter knows that when he thinks about this week ending, a pit grows in his stomach, and it's not just because Aurora has nothing for him anymore or that he dreads facing the music. It's because he already can't imagine his life without Link in it.

"I think we're really good at being fake-married," Carter finishes, because he can't admit to any of those things, because as much as it may feel real, it isn't. "Banker orgies aside," he adds.

Link snorts and kicks Carter's shin. "Goodnight, Carter Jacob."

"Goodnight, Link."

EIGHT

IN THE GRAY DAWN OF the next morning, Carter stands at the French doors of the balcony, where rain pelts the glass and turns the cobblestone street into a rushing river. A single car comes creeping through, sending jets of dirty water spraying in all directions.

"You know," Carter muses to himself. "In Amsterdam, city architects realized early on that, instead of fighting the fact that they lived on a floodplain, they could work with it, building the city based on canals and bridges."

"If you're suggesting we take to the town on a gondola, I am in." Link joins him at the balcony doors, sipping a cup of coffee that fogs the cold window in a little circle. Below, someone, hunched over as the wind and rain whip around them, rushes from one store to another.

"What was on the agenda today?" Carter asks.

"Walking tour of the Garden District."

"Ah," Carter says.

Link turns away from the doors, heads back to the bed, and says over their shoulder, "So. Are you any good at card games?"

The rain continues to pour all morning and into the early afternoon. They play gin rummy and cribbage, then war and go fish. Carter kills at go fish, because Link's expressive face gives away every match. Carter insists on playing poker after that and he cleans Link's clock. Then Link deals cards for something called "Egyptian rat screw."

"You made that up," Carter says, gathering his cards into a neatly fanned pile. "This is not a real a game."

"It is! I learned it from the keyboard player for Chumbawamba when I was kid." Link sets the rest of the cards face down on the bed. "Okay, so the rules are—"

"Wait. Hold on." Carter crosses his legs beneath him. "You're going to have to give me more details on that."

Link only supplies, "I had a weird childhood. Okay, rules!" Link explains the game is similar to war, but numbers match to numbers until a face card is played. If there isn't a face card match, the player who laid it down takes the hand—unless a slap rule comes into place.

"Like a double, or a joker is played. Also if there's four in a row, like a king, queen, ace, two. Or a sandwich: a five then a seven then a five for example. A marriage: king and queen, but for all the queers here in the room, I'm amending that to any king-king, queen-queen, king-queen or ace-royal combination, and oh, we'll make jacks nonbinary! Then there's top-bottom, which is—*Carter.*"

Carter snickers, then apologizes, then snickers again. "Go on."

Link laughs behind the ace of spades. "You're terrible. A top-bottom is—"

"I think the preferred term is 'versatile,'" Carter interjects.

"Oh. My goodness." Link uses the card like a fan, cheeks darkening. "I remember this saucy side of you from that first night. Here I thought it was the absinthe talking."

Carter is feeling a little saucy, perhaps too much time close to Link and Link's pretty eyes and pretty smile and bright laughter. Carter tucks his legs up against his chest and leans away from Link. "I still remember almost nothing from that night."

Something crosses Link's face at that; their silly grin fading and eyes flicking down. "Well, it was a day I'm sure both of us would rather forget."

Carter aches to reach out, to take Link's hand, to pretend that this little world in this cozy hotel room can be real: the two of them and no one else, no lingering presence of Matthew or Jamie. It wouldn't last, but does that matter? He wants to pull Link close, press his lips to the sad, soft curve of Link's lips—

He's staring at Link's mouth. Link notices and blushes again.

"I have to make a phone call!" Carter jumps up from the bed so quickly he stumbles sideways into the wall. "Be right back."

He goes only as far as the stairwell at the end of the carpeted hallway, where he paces on the landing between the fourth and third floors. He calls Paige and has no idea why he would call his sister of all people, only that Paige has this great habit of extinguishing any joy or hope he's ever had. He needs a detached, judgmental, uncaring voice of reason.

"Carter? Are you back home?"

"No. I—" Carter stops pacing and presses his forehead against the cool cement wall. "Please tell me a rebound fling would be a terrible idea, particularly because they would also be having a rebound fling with me, and we'd just be making everything worse. Tell me that what I'm feeling isn't real, it's just loneliness." He waits for her to yell about how stupid he's being, how pathetic, how he's making his life difficult for no reason, as usual.

"Well," she says. "Like, a meaningless fling isn't *always* a bad idea."

Carter spins away from the wall. "Seriously? You choose this moment to experiment with moral ambiguity? And I didn't say meaningless." Whatever confusing feelings he has for Link, they most certainly are not meaningless.

"'Experiment with moral ambiguity.' God, you're so dramatic." *That* is more like her. "So, like, sometimes it can help you get over someone. Matthew left a void inside you, and so maybe someone can fill that void for a little while."

Carter squeezes his eyes closed and pinches at the bridge of his nose. "Paige, that's really inappropriate, and I don't appreciate your references to my sex life," he says diplomatically, tamping down his outrage over her advice.

"Not like that! You're disgusting!"

"No, *you're* disgusting!"

His retort echoes in the hallway, and he recalls why he never talks to Paige about anything personal; suddenly he's six years old again, having a slap fight with his sister in the back of the family SUV while Mom screams at them and swerves all over the road and Dad blanks out as if he's ascended to a different realm where only he exists.

Carter pushes a hand through his hair, focuses on breathing in and out, and finger-combs his hairstyle neatly back into place. "Okay. I have to go. Um, thanks." He starts to hang up, but Paige calls out his name just before he hits the button.

"I meant it. When I said I wanted you to be happy," she says, when he puts the phone back to his ear. "So. Whatever. If this will make you happy, then I think you should go for it."

Maybe, for the first time in her entire life, Paige is right.

Heart pounding, throat dry, Carter makes his way back to the room. If Paige really is right, then comforting each other physically could be exactly what they both need. What if they really could go ahead and get over Matthew and Jamie once and for all, together? Carter is attracted to Link and he's pretty sure now that it's not totally one-sided. He feels comfortable with Link, who is interesting and fun and charismatic, and whose genuine affection and flirtatiousness toward Carter is the only thing keeping his self-esteem from plunging into a free fall. So what if their relationship isn't real? Maybe, for a little while, it could be.

Standing outside the room, Carter decides: He'll propose it. He'll be respectful. He'll just float the idea out there, and if Link wants to, great. If not, also great. He opens to the door to find Link sprawled gracefully on the bed, arms open as if in invitation, mouth quirked into a smile. Urgent heat has already begun to pool in Carter's belly.

His phone rings. Paige, to add her further two cents, naturally. With a sigh, he retrieves his phone from his pocket, intending to toss it into his suitcase. Instead he freezes with his arm stretched out, as if he's afraid to bring the phone any closer.

Link sits up in alarm. "Carter? What is it? Are you okay?"

Carter blinks at them as if emerging from a trance, as if he accidentally got caught in the veil between reality and fantasy and fell right on his face back in reality.

"It's Matthew."

NINE

LINK STANDS. THE PHONE STOPS ringing, then starts again. Matthew's name flashes onto the screen. The phone stops ringing. Matthew's name disappears. Should Carter have blocked him? That seems petty. Of course, Carter will have to speak to him again at some point; they lived together, they at least have to figure out how to navigate that whole minefield. That must be what he wants.

"Are you gonna..." Link says, as Carter tosses the phone on top of a cable-knit sweater in his suitcase. Carter wipes damp hands on his corduroys, then shakes his head to clear it. What was he doing? He was going to proposition Link, that's right. Because they're both lonely castoffs and should fill each other's voids or something. God. That Paige thought it was a good idea should have been his first clue that it is, in fact, a terrible one.

"Hey, are you hungry? I'm starving; let's order room service." Carter plops onto the bed and snags the receiver from the heavy, utilitarian hotel phone.

"Carter, are you okay?" Link swivels, eyebrows pulled low.

"Sure," Carter says. He presses 2 for room service. "Burgers sound good?"

Link nods, then hauls a huge hardside suitcase onto the bed and removes various brightly colored bottles and tubes as Carter orders the food. Link stands and tugs off their long asymmetrical sweater to reveal a tight white T-shirt, then cranks up the heat.

"It'll be forty-five minutes," Carter announces, dropping the phone back into the cradle. He cocks his head at Link, who is now lining up tweezers and brushes, something that looks like a tiny green paint roller, and something else that looks like a tiny vacuum.

"Spa day," Link says to Carter's unasked but obvious question. "You need a spa day." Carter allows himself to be led into the bathroom, where Link nudges him onto the toilet and unfurls a fluffy hotel towel. "You can take your sweater off," Link encourages. Carter scoots awkwardly back, situating himself as well as one possibly can on a closed toilet seat.

"Is that really necessary?" Carter hedges.

Link flaps the towel in the air like a matador's cape. "It's nothing I haven't already seen, Carter Jacob, but suit yourself."

It's not a matter of having seen it before, it's how far Carter allowed himself to think about Link *like that* and how far he now has to yank himself back from the brink. Draping the towel over Carter's sweater, Link sets to work, picking up the paint roller thing first.

"What is that?"

Link holds it up, then presses it to Carter's cheek, rolling it up and down; it's cool and smooth and strange. "*This* is a jade facial roller. Improves circulation and reduces puffiness."

Carter touches his face, worried now. "Am I too puffy?"

"We all are, Carter," Link answers tartly. "We all are."

The proximity is awkward and easy at the same time, too much and not enough: Link's body close to his, Link touching his face and shoulders and smiling down at him. Yet the easy camaraderie returns, and Carter is able to push Matthew's intrusion and his own near-indiscretion down and away.

"You ever had a spa day before?" Link massages moisturizer into Carter's face and then his hands.

Carter swallows when Link's fingers pull at his. He closes his eyes. "Yes, sort of. When my sister can't find anyone else to go she'll take me to get a manicure."

Link *mmhmms*, turning Carter's hand over to rub circles into his palm. It sends little zaps of pleasure up Carter's arm. "What's she like?"

"Paige? She's—" How to describe Paige? Pushy? Judgmental? Opinionated? Mean? "Let's say, she's very forthcoming."

"Interesting." Link snaps open a tube and squeezes green goop onto the vacuum thing, which seems to be an exfoliator. It buzzes and spins on Carter's cheek.

"Why is that interesting?"

"Well," Link says, drawing the word out slowly. "I wouldn't really describe *you* as forthcoming, so I think it's interesting that your sister would be." Link moves the exfoliating tool to Carter's chin, making it difficult for him to respond, not that he knows what to say. Carter is quieter, perhaps not as bluntly and loudly in touch with his feelings as Paige. He's always thought of his reticence as a good thing, a sign of maturity that Paige doesn't possess. But if he held back his true self and real feelings in his relationship, then what chance did he and Matthew really have? It's a lot to unpack for a spa day.

Link wipes off the green goo, then spreads some other goo that dries and tightens as a mask on Carter's skin. "I don't have siblings," Link says, "that I know of."

"Okay, you have got to share more details of your childhood," Carter says, though it's difficult to move his mouth.

"Well." Link flicks their fingers in a casual mock-dismissal. "My mother is sort of the last hanger-on of a hippie movement that ended a couple decades before she got there. She's very... open. And my father works as a road tech for touring musicians, so spending time with him meant being gone somewhere, always moving. We're not very close; sometimes it feels like I don't really know him." Link twists the cap back onto the tube of green goo, mouth pressing into a flat line. "My folks were together but not, if that makes sense."

Link peels the mask away, leaning close to inspect whatever it was supposed to do to Carter's face. They lean back, seemingly satisfied, and Carter scrunches his cheeks and nose and opens and closes his mouth. His skin does feel very fresh.

"Can I shape your eyebrows?" Link asks, snapping tweezers in the air. When Carter nods, they lean in very close, mouth level with Carter's eyes, shining lips, plump and pulled into a pout as Link concentrates, softly parted and—Carter forces his gaze away to his own knees.

"I had a great childhood, don't get me wrong. It was unusual, but—" Link cups one side of Carter's face so their fingers are around his jaw and their thumb presses his temple. With the other hand, they *yank*. Carter winces, closing his eyes. *Ow.*

"Oh, it's not that bad," Link chides, then continues their story. "I couldn't have asked for better parents to be there for me as this artsy, nonbinary, pansexual queer kid, right? I was always accepted and respected. I never lacked for adults who took me seriously and encouraged me and taught me weird card games. I've been all over the U.S. and other parts of the world. Still, there were days I wished for a normal life with a regular, normal family."

Carter winces with every yank of an eyebrow hair. "I—ow—I— *mmh*—had a 'normal, regular' family, and I would have traded places with you in a heartbeat." All his family cares about is appearing as *regular* and *normal* as possible, maintaining the status quo, and keeping up with the Joneses and all that nonsense, and it's made them all miserable.

"I wasn't allowed to watch TV or play video games," Link says.

Carter pretends to shudder. "Never mind."

Link laughs, then savagely yanks another eyebrow hair. "Lately, especially, I've really craved stability. I settled where my roots are and I just really, really wanted someone to share that with. I want a partner. I want commitment. I want someone there for all the regular, boring days and—" Link sets the tweezers onto the counter with a *clack*. "I want something I guess I can't really have."

Link is still standing close, so close. Their legs are between Carter's open legs, and one hand still cradles Carter's face; their eyelids are heavy, and their tongue is wetting their bottom lip. Carter swelters under the towel with his thick sweater still on. He should have taken it off.

Link's shirt is so transparent Carter can see their dark nipples through the fabric. Being with Link, *like that*, would be a bad idea. Right?

"Carter, I want—"

Carter's phone rings from the hallway. Probably Matthew again. As Carter looks toward it, considering whether to pick up, Link packs up the spa day and leaves the bathroom. He wasn't going to answer, he's pretty sure.

What was it that Link wanted? What does Matthew want? And most confusing of all, what does Carter want from either of them?

TEN

CARTER AND LINK EAT THEIR burgers in silence at opposite ends of the tiny room. Matthew's phone calls have punctured their cozy little bubble, whether or not Carter speaks to him again. He still exists, and that's enough.

Carter has to know. "Has Jamie called you?"

Link's head shakes no. *Is it better,* Carter wonders, *being completely forgotten so easily? Or is the repeated and sudden reminder of being left behind the worse scenario?*

"I'm taking a depression nap," Link announces, so Carter, sitting cross-legged on a far corner of the bed, watches the TV on mute and with closed captions on. Two episodes of *This Old House* later, Carter feels his own depression nap coming on, tips over onto his side, and blinks drowsily as the host explains the many uses of C-clamps in home remodeling.

"Gonna get some C-clamps," Carter says to no one. He yawns and pulls the brown blanket around him.

He's in and out of consciousness for another episode and a half, until Link gets up and makes too much noise in the bathroom, then comes out and turns the TV off and a light on.

"Hey." Carter sits up and blinks against the glare. "I was watching that."

Link sets on hand on a hip. "You were fast asleep."

"No." Carter shakes his head, rubs his eyes, blinks at the TV, and says in a sleepy voice, "I really wanted to see them replace that garage door opener."

"I'm sure you did," Link replies, grabbing Carter's wrists and tugging him up, saying curtly, "You're very adorable right now, but I need you to go change into something nice that is also machine washable and stain-resistant."

Carter does as he's told and doesn't ask any follow up questions, because Link called him adorable and it makes him feel squirmy inside in good and bad ways and also because, given the haunted tour and an afternoon at a cemetery, he's afraid to ask *why* he needs stain-resistant, machine washable clothes.

It's still raining on the car ride to wherever they're headed, and the already dark sky shifts darker, into evening. The usual vibrant and vivid city is cast in pallid, somber gray. Neither he nor Link, caught up in the heavy gray mood, speaks at all until the driver drops them off at the end of a narrow city block tightly packed with old brick buildings and a view of the Mississippi River.

"Dumping a body?" Carter guesses, scanning the area from beneath an awning.

Link squints at him, then opens a door leading to a steep staircase too narrow to go up side by side, so Link's rather nice behind ends up right at Carter's eye-level. Carter keeps his eyes trained resolutely on his shoes; he's liable to trip on these stairs anyway. Before Matthew called, Carter might have joked flirtatiously about the current proximity of his face to Link's behind, and Link might have arched a saucy eyebrow and flirtatiously joked back. It might have meant nothing, or it might have meant something, but it would have been a moment that belonged only to him and Link. Instead, they've both been reminded that they really are merely two people who have been cast aside and are still hung up on the ones who left them.

Upstairs is a bright, cheerful room with six chrome-topped kitchen islands that have single-burner cooktops and sinks, and a long front counter with six sets of bowls filled with cooking materials and ingredients.

"A cooking class?" Carter guesses, relieved that his clothes only need to resist sauce stains and not, say, blood.

Link nods and retrieves the bowl of needed items, and the instructor hands Carter two aprons with *Sweetheart Cooking School* embroidered on their fronts. *It's charming*, Carter thinks, as he drapes the apron over his head and Link does the same, though the "a" in "heart" is a tomato, which makes it look as if it reads "Sweetheort."

The rest of the class trickles in, takes their places, and puts on aprons, and the instructor waves and looks appropriately enthusiastic, saying in a strong Louisiana accent, "Hey everyone! Welcome to couples Cajun cooking!"

Couples? Stomach sinking, Carter looks around. At every station, he sees people holding hands or giving one another loving touches on arms or backs, soft smiles, and sweet glances.

"Couples Cajun cooking?" Carter hisses. The instructor informs them they're making gumbo and starting with something called a "roux."

Link shrugs. "When we planned it, I thought it was a little touristy, and probably not authentic, but it was also expensive, so that's something."

"Not the—" Carter is interrupted by a whisking demonstration and then six whisks all going at once. One couple is even whisking *together*. "The couple thing, I meant."

Link whisks and rolls their eyes and whisks faster. "I thought that would be obvious." The instructor moves on—and then the class moves on—to chopping celery.

"Well, I wish you would have said," Carter says, louder over the racket. "I could have mentally prepared myself."

Link stops chopping and loudly replies, "It's not like we have to make out in front of the entire class, Carter," just as everyone else stops chopping and the room goes silent, waiting for further instruction. Eleven people turn in their direction. Carter wants to fling himself into the nearby river. Link smiles and says without missing a beat, "This isn't *that* kind of class, right?" The class titters, and Link resumes chopping.

Carter was caught unawares, is all. And he's still kind of sleepy. And he maybe has feelings for Link that are complicated by the fact that he was dumped by his fiancé and hasn't let himself feel anything about that, let alone figure out what his feelings for Link might mean. "I'm sorry," Carter says. He's sorry for a lot of things lately.

"It's fine," Link says, accepting the apology with a frown and averted eyes. "I get caught up in my own head sometimes. I should have told you before we came here. Just mince the garlic, please."

Carter minces garlic and takes over vegetable chopping duties while Link whisks the roux. Link, keeping a close eye on the color and texture of the mixture until it's a smooth deep brown, looks comfortable and confident while cooking. Link takes it off the heat and whisks a little longer, before the instructor tells them to.

"You seem to know what you're doing," Carter says, trying to make peace.

Link coyly lifts one shoulder. "I do make a pretty passable gumbo."

Together they mince the veggies and add them to the roux, and then the big pot goes back on the burner. "Do you like to cook?" Carter asks.

Link nods, glancing up and then away. Steam twists and climbs, flushing Link's cheeks and lips a deep red. "Sometimes. When I was a kid, I'd stay with my granny for a few weeks in the summer. She loved to cook, like classic Louisiana cuisine: jambalaya, red beans and rice, shrimp and grits, gumbo. You?"

"Sometimes," Carter echoes. "I didn't really have anyone willing to teach me. I love to bake, though. The second it hits fall weather, I haul out the mini-cupcake tins and festive sprinkles."

Link's mouth curls into a gentle smile, reaching out with a soft touch to Carter's bent elbow, and says, "Just when I think you can't get any cuter." Which is funny, because Carter was thinking the same thing.

Then Link moves closer and grabs the handle of the knife Carter is still using. "Okay, you have clearly never properly prepared okra; let me help."

ELEVEN

ON THE ITINERARY FOR THE next day is a ride on the St. Charles streetcar, where the tracks lead beyond the French Quarter into uptown and around the Riverbend in the most historic parts of the city. Link is quiet at breakfast and on the walk to the trolley and as they sit next to Carter on a small wooden trolley bench. Quiet, but not sad. *Contemplative*, Carter thinks. Carter himself has no desire to contemplate anything, having successfully stomped all of his feelings away again. He's distracted by all the sights as the little green trolley slowly chugs along on the tracks. Several large mansions with a delightful mix of sprawling European splendor and traditional Southern antebellum symmetry pass by. Carter yammers on about the hallmarks of antebellum neoclassical architecture from Jackson Avenue to all the way to the end of the line.

Before taking the streetcar back, they stop for po'boys and crawfish étouffée and beers at a restaurant in the Riverbend neighborhood, sitting on the deck outside even though it's a little too chilly. It's nowhere near as chilly as Aurora will be, though. Carter's time in New Orleans and with Link is coming to an end, and, though "vibrant" was never really a word he would have used to describe Aurora, after being here he can only imagine his world back home painted in various shades of lifeless beige.

Link takes him to the aquarium, then the Audubon garden, and then they make a stop at the Spanish fountain with its colorful tiles and a picturesque view of the river. Link pauses in front of the fountain to check something on their phone. Their scarf and hair are gently tousled by the wind; they're dressed casually today in striped blue pants and a loose white button-up. The sun sets, orange and pink, behind them; the fountain sparkles jewels. Nothing can capture how Link looks in this instant, nothing can make it last longer than a few beats of Carter's heart. Carter's hand twitches toward his phone to take a picture, but instead he tries to mentally snap this perfect moment. Link's head turns to direct a wide smile Carter's way, and that moment is better still.

At the French Market, a vendor fast-talks Carter into buying a Mardi Gras mask and beads and a New Orleans snow globe with a plastic gator, riverboat, and Bourbon Street signpost inside. Link judges him appropriately for his tacky souvenirs, then hands him a bag as they wait together on the corner for a ride back to the hotel. Then they'll head on to a jazz club for the night's agenda. "Got you something."

Carter opens the bag to find a birdhouse made in the style of a New Orleans cottage home. It's pastel yellow with pale green shutters and a bright blue door.

"It even has a little fleur-de-lis gable on the porch," Link points out. "The vintage house you always wanted."

Carter is so touched, he can't do more than nod and run his finger over all the perfect little details on the perfect little house.

Then it's a stop at the hotel, just long enough to drop stuff off and change clothes. Carter switches from one plaid button-down and sweater to a different plaid button-down and sweater and Link changes from the simple white shirt and blue pants to—

"Wow."

With a grin, Link spins in place, wearing a skintight, midriff-baring black T-shirt, virtually painted-on leather pants, and heavy black eyeliner. "Yeah?"

"Yeah. Wow," Carter repeats. "I feel a little…" He looks at his slacks and dress shirt and frowns. "Boring," he decides.

Suddenly peppy and once again bright, Link waves him off, slips on heeled black boots, says, "You look as cute as always," pats Carter's cheek, and leads the way out of the room.

"I look like a JC Penney catalogue model," Carter says as they cross the ornate lobby and head outside. "Not in a good way. In a boring, bland-looking-so-everyone-notices-the jeans-on-sale-for-$12.99-instead-of-the-model sort of way."

Link snaps their fingers and says, teasing, "Oh my—that's it! Was driving me crazy." They open the car door and gesture for Carter to get in. After climbing in next to him, Link pats Carter's knee and bumps their shoulder against Carter's. "I like that about you."

"That I'm boring?"

"No." Link laughs. "That you're so much more than what you seem on the outside. I think you're one of the most fascinating people I've ever known."

Carter shakes his head. "Me?" Link must not know very many people.

"Yes, you," Link says. It's not a very long drive, and soon the car is pulling into a busy street with lights flashing all colors of the rainbow and music pumping. "Thanks to you, what should have been the worst week of my life has been pretty wonderful. *You* have been wonderful." The car stops, and Link turns with an impossibly fond smile. Rainbow lights sweep across the car's interior; Link's hand is still on Carter's knee. "And now I'm over it. Jamie, the wedding, all of it."

Carter stares at Link's hand, fingers curved on his kneecap, thumb just a little higher on his thigh. *Over it.* "Just like that?"

Link's head tilts. "Just like that. I felt what I need to feel, maybe you should—"

Link doesn't finish saying what Carter should maybe do; instead, they step out of the car and walk around to hold Carter's door open. "What should I do?" Carter says, but the street party engulfs him, and his question is swallowed up in the celebratory vortex. Carter has to lean right next to Link's ear to be heard over the commotion. "I thought Mardi Gras was next week?"

"Consider it pregaming!" Link shouts back. "Only with more alcohol *and* more nudity."

Up and down Bourbon Street, the pre-Mardi Gras party rages with an abundance of drinking and dancing and skin. Carter is gobsmacked; he's been to parties, but nothing like this. It's alive and intoxicating and, as he stands next to Link who is just as electrifying, a charge zaps up his spine, seeps into his blood, and hums along his skin. The next time the crowd *wooos*, Carter *wooos* along. Link disappears, then reappears with a hurricane in a plastic cup as tall as Carter's arm is long. Someone flings beads into the crowd from a balcony, and everyone screams. A string of glittery gold beads lands next to Carter's shoe. The street party's ebullience is intoxicating.

"Carter!" Link shouts, close to Carter's face. "You should *feel* whatever you need to *feel*! Stop holding back!"

Carter blinks. "Okay." He presses a hard, closed-mouth kiss to Link's lips. Around them, the crowd erupts into cheers while shining beads clatter down like rain. He's leaving and he may never see Link again. It's now or never.

The wildest party Carter has ever witnessed rages on around them, but right now all that exists is his mouth on Link's mouth. Nothing else matters. No one else matters.

TWELVE

CARTER PULLS BACK FROM THE kiss. The taste of strawberry lip gloss is still sweet on his lips. His mouth is tingly, and his heart pounds. The kiss felt like an exhale. Link stares, frozen, fingers raised to their mouth, trembling across their open lips.

Carter starts to form an apology, to say he was caught up in a moment. But never has a moment felt so right. Unless Link didn't—

Link grabs Carter by the back of the head and crashes their mouths together. It's nothing like the first kiss. It's hungry and open and biting and they only pull away, gasping for air, when the crowd moves and Link is shoved accidentally, moving them bodily away. Carter reaches for them and has a sudden flash of that first night, the first time they were both drunk and partying. Something is so familiar about this moment:

The strawberry lip gloss.

Link's sweetly curved mouth.

Carter reaching, so sure of the rightness of it.

The world spinning around Carter as if everything had shifted.

Link hooks an arm around Carter's shoulders to keep him close, then says, pressed chest to chest and cheek to cheek, "Fuck, *finally*." Together they dance, draping beads over each other's necks, and kiss and kiss, lips sweet and skin hot and hands daring. Back at the hotel, pressed against the door, Carter skirts his fingertips along Link's warm sides and up beneath their shirt, dragging along curving hips and flat belly and angled ribs and the dip of their lower back.

"Is this okay?" Carter asks in a whisper, running his fingers just over the top of Link's pants, just at the edge of seeking more.

"Yes," Link asks, smiling against Carter's tender lips. "So polite."

Carter curves his hands over Link's ass, kneading and rubbing but not pulling in, letting Link decide what to do. Link kisses down Carter's neck and jaw, shoves a leg between Carter's. Carter groans, pleasure unspooling through his body, nothing urgent, like the lazy roll of the Mississippi. Carter is buzzed but not drunk, not like the first night he met Link, just enough to take the edge off and not think, not so much that he won't remember. Link takes Carter's hands, walking backward and tugging Carter along.

Falling into bed together is something they have done every night for the past week as strangers pretending to be lovers. No more pretending. Carter shoves away the wall of pillows that kept him barricaded from Link and feels no embarrassment when he presses the length of his body against Link's, touching Link in a way he'd only allowed himself to imagine in dreams.

"Is this okay?" Carter asks again. It's been so long since he learned someone's body for the first time: what makes them gasp and squirm in pleasure, what their limits are. Carter grinds down on Link's thigh, slides his own leg between Link's.

"Yes," Link says, on a gasp into Carter's mouth, rubbing against him and clutching Carter's shoulders.

It's perfect—kissing and grinding and touching without holding anything back—until it isn't; the slow-burning pleasure turns into urgent need. Link pulls back first, breathing out, "Wait," then struggling out of the tiny, sexy, skintight shirt.

Link's skin is soft and smells faintly of coconuts. Carter tastes Link's neck and shoulders, those gorgeously curved collarbones and the soft hollow between. Link's gasps turn into soft moans; their hips twist sideways to pin Carter's leg. Link's back arches. The new position puts Carter's lips closer to the center of their chest, right at one dusky nipple. It seems to be a silent request, but just to be sure Carter bends slowly, looking up at Link's blissed-out face. "Please," Link says, then cups the back of Carter's head and nudges it forward.

Carter licks flat across one nipple, then the other, circles both until a hard nub forms, and then flicks the tip of his tongue against them. Link gasps, hips rubbing down hard, back bowing even farther. When Carter sets his lips around one nipple, sucks and flicks his tongue against the nub while pinching and rubbing the other, Link's thrusting grows erratic; their deep groans turn into sweet, high whines. The hand on Carter's head grips his hair, keeping Carter in place and his mouth and tongue and fingers in motion until Link goes quiet, grinds down one more time, and then goes still and rigid.

Link tips Carter's face up, bends to kiss him messily, and trembles with weak full-body spasms and a smile that curves against Carter's lips. Ridiculously turned on after feeling and watching Link come, Carter shifts to rub himself to completion. *Dry-humping,* Link called it, and which Carter has been under-appreciating as mere foreplay.

But Link squirms out from beneath him and off the bed, then struggles out of the tight, tight leather pants, down to only bright red briefs. Carter opens his pants and shoves his underwear down, pulling at himself just to get a little relief.

Link puts their hair into a messy topknot; a condom packet is clenched between their front teeth. Hair satisfactorily up, Link plucks the condom out and holds it up, cocking one hip and saying, "I'd like to go down on you, or would you rather just do that? I'm happy to watch." They nod to Carter's hand on himself.

Carter can't imagine a scenario in which he'd say no to Link's gorgeous, pouty lips around him and wants to ask how Link could ask such a dumb question. He also wants to be respectful, so he stops touching himself, pushes up onto his elbows, and politely requests, "I'd like for you to go down on me, please."

Link laughs, beckoning Carter forward to the edge of the bed before dropping between Carter's bent legs. "Only you could politely request oral sex and still be cute."

Only Link could call me cute while putting a condom on me, Carter thinks, but does not say. He's having trouble saying much besides "yes," over and over. He doesn't want to dwell too much on the newness of Link's mouth on him, that it's someone else, someone different, but it's impossible not to. Link isn't particularly methodical, which is new, and is very enthusiastic, which is new and nice. Method hardly matters, though. It feels amazing, and Carter is so wound up that he comes without warning, before he can get a word out about being close.

After showers and tidying up and climbing into bed, Carter rests his cheek against Link's shoulder and drapes his arm over Link's torso with a hand splayed on the curve of their belly. Carter soon becomes so comfortable and content he's barely clinging to consciousness. And then Link says his name as though it's a question.

"Mmph?" Carter manages.

Link huffs a little laugh and shifts to kiss the top of Carter's head. "Never mind. It doesn't matter." Carter yawns, shifts, and scoots even closer. As he's dropping off to sleep, Link mumbles something; their voice slides into Carter's hazy mind like a subliminal message as he hovers between awareness and dreaming. "Do not dwell in the past, do not dream of the future, concentrate the mind on the present moment."

THIRTEEN

CARTER STRETCHES OUT ON HIS back, still naked, after a very satisfying night's sleep. He's alone, woken by the sound of a door closing. Link must have gone to the bathroom. It's Carter's last day here, there's still so much of New Orleans that he wants to see and experience, and now that he and Link have gone from pretend lovers to real lovers, he can only imagine the extra infusion of joy and excitement the day will have. Maybe he'll hold Link's hand and walk the river, then finally do that Garden District tour where he can ramble on about double gallery houses and center-hall cottages and how to spot the telltale architectural differences between Italianate, Greek Revival, and Queen Anne mansion styles.

Carter pulls clothes for the day from his suitcase, noticing that the bathroom is dark and empty. Link must have gone out for one last beignet run, then. Maybe Carter can kiss the powdered sugar off their lips, taste the sweet chicory-coffee flavor of café au lait on Link's tongue. But after Carter showers and dresses and shaves, Link still isn't back. Café Du Monde isn't far from the hotel. Maybe there's a line. Link knows a locals-only shortcut to the checkout. It's never taken this long.

He sits on the balcony to people-watch and soak up the city for a little longer, but it makes him too sad about leaving, so he goes back inside. His home has become a cross to bear and a city he's spent a week in has become the only source of light in his life: New Orleans and Link. Carter shakes himself out of the thought. One more day. He doesn't have to think about Matthew, or the condo he'll find emptied of Matthew's things, or going back to work and everyone's questions, or his dead-end life or his soul-sucking family. He turns on the TV, but finds nothing of interest.

Where the hell is Link?

Someone knocks on the door, and Carter hops up in relief, then deflates when he realizes that Link has a key and wouldn't need to knock, then gets his hopes up again when he reasons that they could have forgotten it. It's room service with the last honeymoon-special breakfast.

"Have you happened to see my…" Carter cranes his neck to look past the concierge, glancing left and right down the hallway. "Partner? Anywhere?"

"No, sorry." The concierge holds a hand out for their tip.

Carter doesn't want to eat alone, but he's hungry and really starting to worry, so he stress-eats a mini quiche and four toast points. It's only after he puts the tray in the hall outside the room, after the food has long gone cold, that it finally dawns on him: Link's many toiletries are cleared off the counter; shampoo and conditioner and coconut body wash are gone from the shower. No black sharp-heeled boots or heavy combat boots or purple high-top sneakers sit at the bottom of the closet. He opens the stupid armoire that takes up nearly half the tiny room and—empty.

Carter stands in place until the room spins and sways too much for him to stay on his feet. The bed is still messily undone on both sides, but Link's pillow is against the headboard where they must have sat propped up after waking. Carter's breakfast turns bitter in his stomach. He stands again, smooths the sheets, and puts the pillows in place. On Link's side of the bed, a notepad has been removed from the bedside drawer and a pen set beside it. One word is written beneath the hotel's logo:

Carter,

His name and a comma, as if Link had planned to go on but didn't, wanted to give Carter an explanation and then didn't find it necessary. Link is gone, and Carter is alone. Alone, all alone.

He's alone.

It crashes over him like panic, like panic but emptier, like despair but sharper. Carter claps a hand over his heart and reminds his ribs to expand and his lungs to pull air and his heart to slow. He's fine. He's fine, he's fine, he's fine.

Still frozen at the side table with the notepad clutched in one hand, Carter looks at his feet to center himself and spots a blue hair tie that's been dropped between the bed and the table. It's the blue hair tie Link used last night. It could have been a dream, the whole thing, if not for these two last, insignificant points connecting him to Link. In his suitcase, the cottage birdhouse is tucked safely away. He has the room for the night; he could stay and see the things he missed by himself. He could.

Instead, Carter books a new flight home, pays the exorbitant cost for something leaving today as soon as possible, and then calls for a cab and packs the rest of his things.

"Paige?" Carter wheels his suitcase behind him with his phone tucked between his ear and shoulder. "I'm coming back tonight and I need you to do me a favor." When Paige replies that she won't do anything without getting something herself first, he's ready, because of course she won't. The door slams behind him. Carter walks to the elevator. "I'll go out with your friend," he says.

It's over, really over. All of it. It's time for Carter to move on.

FOURTEEN

OVER THE NEXT TWO WEEKS, Carter finds that, if he sleeps with his legs dangling off the end of the cramped two-seater couch in his office, he doesn't wake up with a crick in his neck. It takes a good ten minutes for the pins and needles in his legs to dissipate, but at least he can turn his neck from side to side without excruciating pain.

Carter sits up on the couch before dawn, his routine now, stretching aching muscles and rubbing his shins. His office has one narrow window running along the top of one wall. There was a time he was proud of earning this office with that window, a moment when he'd picked out this hard, gray-blue couch from a corporate catalogue and thought: *Yes, this is what I want.* Wincing at a sharp pain in his back as he stands to face the day, Carter no longer knows who that guy was—the one who chose this couch and this office, who was satisfied with this particular drab lot in life—but he is really starting to hate him.

It's snowing. It's the first day of March. Just to torture himself, Carter checks the weather in New Orleans; it is sunny with a high in the mid-seventies. Of course. Carter changes into the last outfit in a duffel bag that's been shoved into a bottom drawer of his desk and sneaks out of the office building before the day starts for anyone else.

"It's like you're trying to be as pathetic as possible."

He'd asked three small favors of Paige: to let him do laundry and shower at her place, to keep her opinions about his personal life to herself, and to not tell anyone that he's been sleeping at his office. Two out of three was more than he was expecting of her.

"I'm just trying to—"

"Figure out your next steps, yeah, yeah. On that note..."

Paige and Carter are a matching set: brown hair and brown eyes and dimpled smiles, two years apart almost exactly. As kids they were always dressed in coordinating outfits for their yearly family portrait, smiling innocently, two precious cherubs, as if they didn't spend every other waking hour at each other's throats. Matching in looks, they are opposite in personality, even now, in their late twenties. In darker moments, Carter sometimes hopes he'll go bald, if only to stop looking so much like Paige.

Paige works as a sales rep for a pharmaceutical company and spends her weekends hanging with her "girls," who all dress and act eerily like her: a Borg collective of black leggings and puffy vests and hair styled in beachy waves. And that's one reason, among many other reasons, that Carter has no interest in dating any of them. However, he does owe her, and she *hasn't* yet poured bleach onto any of his clothes.

Paige hops up onto the dryer, blocking his efforts to load his clothes with her crossed legs. He scowls at her, but she's on her phone and mostly ignoring him. "You should finally go out with Meredith tomorrow. She's been very patient, Carter." He shoves her legs aside to throw in a pile of wet clothes. "Like, she actually likes you and *still* wants to go out with you even though you're homeless."

"I am not homeless!" Carter yanks the next load out of the washer too quickly; three socks plop onto the floor. "I just don't feel like going home."

"You know he called me. Matt." Paige glances up from texting; she's baiting him.

"Good for Matt." Carter slams the dryer door shut. Paige tucks her legs out of the way just in time, gives him a dark look, and jumps down.

"You are so immature, Carter," she says, as if her own maturity didn't peak in the seventh grade. Carter repeats her in a mocking tone. She rolls her eyes. "Fine, be immature and alone for the rest of your life; see if I care," Paige walks into her bedroom, texting as she goes.

"Fine, I will!" Carter shouts after her. The bedroom door slams. Carter blows out a breath and drops onto her couch, which is large and comfortable and soft, but he'd rather sleep on a bed of nails than ask Paige if he can stay with her. He can't storm out, though, not until his clothes are done, so he flips through a *Cosmo* and waits. In two weeks, he's done almost everything he needs to do in order to extricate what very little is left of his own life from his life with Matthew: The joint bank account has been closed, the wedding cancelled, and his sizable portion of the wedding and honeymoon fund is now in a savings account; everyone at work knows; their friends know; and their friends have chosen a side, and it's not Carter's. In the story of true love finally winning out, Carter was dispensable, a bump in the road.

And to Link, he was—what? Was he anything at all?

Paige swishes out of her bedroom and into the kitchen, bangs around, and then shouts from inside the pantry, "Let's go get Mexican food! I need a margarita or four." She laughs hysterically at her own joke.

Carter rolls his eyes, then stumbles on an article titled, "These Couples Get Real About Wedding Night Sex!" He closes the magazine. "I'll go out with Meredith tomorrow."

"Thank god," Paige says, struggling into thigh-high, fur-lined, suede snow boots. They look brand new. A lot of the shoes piled in the closet look brand new. "You can finally disappoint her, and she'll stop talking about how cute you are and making me gag."

Carter retrieves his own sensible, functional waterproof boots, ties the laces, stands, and waits with an eyebrow raised and arms crossed while Paige continues to try to get one foot in one boot. "It snowed three inches, Paige. It's not the tundra."

"Your face is the tundra," she replies, then cheers when she finally conquers one ridiculous boot. "So, Tapas Tapas or La Casita? My treat."

*   *   *

HE DOES NOT HAVE A terrible time on his date with Meredith. Actually, it's quite nice. She works in event planning, so they have a great time comparing out-of-touch and impossible-to-please nightmare clients all through dinner at a decent Italian place. When the conversation turns to his recent breakup, she's sympathetic and nonjudgmental.

"All I got in my divorces were the dogs and lawyer fees." Meredith tips back another glass of red wine. "Well, that and a lifetime of bitterness. Trust me, you dodged a bullet."

"Maybe," Carter says, swirling his own wine around in the glass. "What I'm struggling with now is, how can I ever trust my own feelings again? What does love even look like?"

Meredith laughs, "Love is bullshit. And so are prenups if your lawyer sucks." She clinks their glasses, then holds hers aloft for another refill.

Later, Carter walks her to her front porch to say goodnight. "I had a good time," he says, standing one step down. He wouldn't mind hanging out again.

Fishing her keys from her purse, Meredith holds his gaze and says, "It doesn't have to end yet." She bites her bottom lip. Her dogs yap incessantly behind the closed door.

"Oh," Carter says. "Uh." She's attractive, though there isn't really a spark, not like with Link. Not that the spark with Link mattered much in the end. He could. He could just sleep his way through enough not-terrible, attractive-enough dates until he can no longer remember what it was like to be with Link or Matthew. If love is bullshit, then what does it matter?

"I—actually, I have to work on some scale models tomorrow. Gonna take all day, so." It wouldn't be right to use Meredith like that. Also, the dogs are already giving him a headache. "Thanks for the nice evening; we should do it again." He half-jogs, half-walks down the driveway.

He still believes in love, despite everything, because he's a fool. And, driving back to spend another night sleeping on the horrible, tiny couch in his office, Carter knows without a doubt that he is exactly as pathetic as Paige says he is.

FIFTEEN

EVERY NIGHT THE SECURITY GUARD for the office building watches Carter spread a pillow and blanket on the couch in his office, and every night Carter watches the security guard smoke a joint in the breezeway outside his window. He likes to think they have an unspoken agreement, or else the security guard simply does not give a shit. Tonight, Carter sits on the edge of his desk, his head in his hands, his mind spinning.

There's a knock. "You were out late tonight." The security sticks his head in the door like a concerned father, though he is definitely younger than Carter and definitely stoned. His name tag says *Stan*.

"Yeah, I had a date," Carter replies, unsure why he's explaining himself to Stan the stoned security guard. Across from his desk is a shelf, and in the middle of his books on architecture Carter has placed the New Orleans cottage birdhouse that Link gave him. The yellow and blue and green stand out against the neutral color scheme in his office. Every time the house catches Carter's eye, which is often, a bright warmth flushes through Carter's body.

"Hey, Stan," Carter calls as Stan starts to leave. "Do you happen to have another one of those joints?"

The small, high windows turn out to be very convenient for blowing smoke outside until the joint is down to just the roach, and Carter sprawls on the floor. Stan lies back across Carter's desk, making a mess of his files and the plans he was working on. Carter is floating, untethered from reality. This is what he's been most afraid of admitting, that he's directionless and drifting. It's not that he's figuring out what to do next as he told Paige; it's that he has no next. He can't go home, because the condo no longer is home. He doesn't want to get a new place here, because he doesn't want to be here. Carter belongs nowhere and with no one. He really is a fool. Just like the fool on the tarot card he filched from a fortune-teller while blitzed on absinthe.

"The thing is," Carter says, as if they were in the middle of a conversation, "I wasn't just lonely. If I was lonely and just wanted *that*, I could be doing *that* with Meredith right now." He checks the time, then amends, "I could have *done that* with Meredith."

"True," Stan says, as if he knows exactly what Carter is talking about. Maybe he does. Maybe they're connecting on some higher wavelength. *Higher.* Carter giggles, then continues, "But Link's messed up, and I'm messed up, and—*left at the altar*. That's *heavy*." Carter can physically feel the weight pressing on him, hitting him over and over in the chest. Oh, wait, no. That's his heart, hammering frantically.

Carter sits up, and the room spins. He can feel his pulse through his whole body. "But I was just a fling for Link because they needed to get over Jamie. I have to accept that. Everyone just takes what they need from ol' Carter, and then they just toss me aside. Doesn't matter what I want. That's just who I am, Toss Aside Carter." This sad fact strikes him as hilarious, and he and Stan laugh and laugh until Stan turns suddenly sober, gets off the desk, and yanks Carter to his feet.

"Listen. Look. Listen, dude." He jabs Carter in the chest and it reverberates like a sonic boom through Carter's body. "Before I got this job, I worked as a mall cop, right. And when I took this job, everyone thought I was nutso, right? They were all, 'Stan, you've got it made! You got a Segway. Pepper spray *and* mace. You can get a hot dog on a stick anytime you want.' No one *got* why I wanted this job instead. And it got *to* me." He taps his own temple. "Like I couldn't believe my own self anymore. But they were wrong. I got it made here. More money, I'm basically my own boss. I got a taser. You understand what I'm saying?"

Carter shakes his head slowly. "No." His brain is sloshing around inside his skull. "No, I do not."

Stand holds Carter's face between his hands, squishing his cheeks. "I am saying…" He says, then squints. "What was I saying…"

With his head held at this angle, Carter is staring right at the birdhouse cottage, vibrant even in his dark, dull office.

"Oh!" Stan says, squishing Carter's cheeks even harder. "I was saying, sometimes you gotta listen to that little voice that's guiding you somewhere. Listen to yourself; forget everyone else. Forget what they want. What do you want, uh… I dunno your name."

Do what I want. What does he want? He can't look away from the birdhouse. What is the birdhouse trying to tell him? What *is* his name? He gasps, eyes wide, and grips Stan's wrists. "Carter. My name is Carter, and I know what I want. I gotta go."

His decision could probably wait until tomorrow instead of occurring at midnight, which it is by the time Carter sobers up enough to drive. But it feels urgent and silly, too, that he's put it off for two weeks. It's just that this is it, the final break. Once he does this, he has no choice but to accept that he has to start over somehow. Until a little while ago, thanks to Stan and half a joint, he didn't know what starting over meant for him. Now he'll be starting his brand-new life on his own terms. And he knows exactly where.

Carter takes a breath, turns his key in the lock, and doesn't exhale until he can see that the condo is quiet and dark and no one is home. Looking around as if he's never been here before, he sets his keys and phone on the counter. Someone has been packing without him; boxes are stacked along the walls in the kitchen, dining area, and living room. Some of the furniture is covered with moving sheets. Some of it is gone.

Paige texts him while he's looking through the cabinets. The cups are all packed. The plates and bowls are not. He starts a new box.

Paige: *I told u to disappoint Mer not piss her off >:{*

He types back: *Packing up my old place right now. Didn't want to sleep with Meredith.*

Paige: *EW TMI*

Carter rolls his eyes and ignores the rest of her texts until he's finished packing the kitchen. It feels good. Necessary. He moves on to the bedroom after grabbing his phone from the counter and continues to ignore the texts from his sister that are still coming in, rapid-fire. He opens the door and stops short. The bedroom is mostly untouched; just the bookshelves are empty. The bed is even made up. *Have they been here?* Carter wonders. Have they been sleeping in this bed, together, the same one Carter and Matthew used to share?

Carter banishes the thought. He's not here for Matthew; he's here for himself. Carter packs the rest of his clothes. It will be nice to not wear the same six outfits anymore. The top middle drawer is filled with stray ties and handkerchiefs, a box of condoms, and a pair of suspenders he never wears. Behind that is the random stuff that was collected over the life of his relationship with Matthew. His phone goes off again, and again, and again. Paige's texts read:

Matt is so ugh

Mer is very open minded. JSYK

Should I tell him where u r?

Just tell Matt 2 f off and b done w it

Or I will

ANSWER ME

CARTER

Mer's last boyfriend was gay

And then three devil emojis flash on his screen, all sent one at a time. With a heavy sigh, Carter texts back: *No! Don't tell Matthew anything* and *Please stop texting like a twelve-year-old.* Her second-to-last text is so obnoxious, and confusing, he doesn't even know where to start.

Carter silences his phone, then scans all the items he stuck in this drawer during his seven years with Matthew, stuff he didn't know what do to with then and doesn't know what to do with now: show programs and concert tickets, ribbons from marathons they completed together, anniversary cards, photos, a vial of sand—

"Carter."

Matthew is standing in the doorway. Carter blinks, then turns away, goes into the attached bathroom to get a trash can, and says nothing as he grabs the items that are attached to so many memories and throws them by the fistful into the trash.

"Remember that?" Matthew says, coming closer. "The sand. St. Barts, that was fun. Remember, on the beach, how we—"

"Don't," Carter says. He throws the sand vial extra hard into the trash can.

"Carter, come on." Matthew turns on the bedroom light; it makes Carter want to hiss and slither into a dark corner. He was supposed to be unburdening himself of this place, and of Matthew, alone. Matthew comes closer again. "Can't we be civil?"

"Civil." Carter snorts and tosses another handful of junk. "That's all we ever were, Matthew. Polite. Reasonable. Fucking—*civil*."

Matthew leans in closer. "Carter, are you high?"

"No," Carter scoffs, hunching his shoulders and turning away. "A little."

"Carter," Matthew says again, gently, reaching out to stop Carter's angry de-hoarding of his junk drawer. "We should talk. I've been worried about you."

This is why it was so easy to fall for Matthew, why Carter ignored all the red flags, why he pushed on through all the moments when he knew he would never be enough for Matthew and that they didn't love each other the way they wanted to, why Carter bent and changed and acquiesced in so many ways in order to keep him. This is why all their friends chose Matthew and not him.

Matthew is so pleasant, so charming. A natural born leader, with confidence to spare. The guy who tells the best stories, makes everyone laugh, is effortlessly likable. Wasn't Carter so lucky to have him? But Matthew needs people to like him, and the worst thing Carter can do is hang Matthew out to dry, make him the bad guy, let him stew impotently in Carter's anger. It's what he should have done in the first place, back in a New Orleans hotel when Matthew confessed that he was in love with someone else.

Carter snatches his hands away. "Talk? Let me think…" He taps his chin and pretends to consider having a civil conversation with Matthew. "Mmm, nope." Carter turns back to his task.

"Okay, you are obviously not in your right mind, so why don't you get some sleep, and we'll talk tomorrow." Matthew starts to walk from the room. Carter won't be here tomorrow or any day after that. Perhaps he's being immature and petty—and is a little high still—but he wants to wound Matthew, make him feel exactly as bereft and rejected as Carter felt when he watched Matthew pull off his engagement ring. All his bottled-up anger finally comes uncorked.

"I loved you," Carter shouts, clutching to his chest a handful of wilted flowers and a ribbon from a 5K they did together two years ago. He doesn't even like running stupid marathons; that was Matthew's thing. "I was dedicated to you! I gave you everything and you left me. You—" He slams the ribbon and flowers into the trash. "You *left* me."

Matthew turns back. He looks regretful and sad and says, softly, "You told me to go."

"What was I supposed to say, Matt?" Carter asks, incredulous. "No, stay with me, I'm happy to be the person you've settled for?"

Matthew deflates; his expression is pained. *Good.* "Tell me what I can do. How can I make this better for you? How can we fix this?"

"No, don't do that. You don't want to make me feel better, you want to unload your own guilt. Well, you can keep it." He tapes up the box of his clothes and a few personal items and dumps the rest of the drawer into the trash. "You can keep all of this. I hope you and Jamie are *very* happy together." He pushes the box to the front door. Matthew follows him. "Goodbye," Carter says, gathering his keys and wallet. "Adios, au revoir, auf—shoot what is it?" He opens the door and shoves his box into the hall. *The German one, what is it?* "Oh. Auf wiedersehen, that's it."

"Carter, can you please—" Matthew says, as Carter tries to remember if he knows how to say "so long, sucker" in any language. "We aren't together, exactly."

Carter pauses. "What?"

Matthew rubs his face and groans. "Me and Jamie, we aren't… it's… complicated. Can you please just come back inside?" His eyes turn pleading; his entire body slumps with misery. Carter wanted to hurt him, but he didn't want to make him *miserable*. "Stay here tonight," Matthew implores, "let's talk this out. Please, Carter?"

SIXTEEN

"Well, what did you say?"

Carter and Paige sit at adjacent tables getting manicures at Paige's favorite salon, after "her girls" had to cancel at the last minute. Manicures with his irritating sister aren't Carter's favorite way of spending a Sunday morning, but Paige also treated him to brunch, and Carter will probably never possess the strength of will to say no to brunch under any circumstances. So here he is, two mimosas and an eggs Benedict later, getting a paraffin treatment.

"I didn't say anything," Carter replies as Babette, the efficient yet rough beauty technician, yanks his hands from a tub of hot wax. "I booked it out of there. Well, as fast as one can book it while pushing a heavy, huge box down a hallway and a stairwell and then through the snow to my car." Babette covers his wax-coated hands in big, soft mittens. "Anyway, even if I did want to work things out with Matthew, it's too late. I've been approved to work remotely for an interim period. I emptied my savings account and I'm meeting a real estate agent in New Orleans on Tuesday for a house I've already put earnest money down on. It's too late," Carter says again. *It is, right?*

"We'll let the moisture really penetrate the epidermis," Babette tells him, turning her attention to neatly arranging the various bottles on the table.

"Um," Carter replies.

"You're totally gonna go crawling back to him," Paige says. She's getting her nails filed; her arms are stretched across the table. "You'll go back to Matthew because you're weak and he's got you on the hook."

She pulls her hands away long enough to mime cranking a fishing pole. "You'll do whatever he wants."

"Wow, Paige," Carter deadpans. "Tell me how you really feel." The mimosas were not worth this. "I wish I could talk to Link about it," he says to his mitten-covered hands. Link would get it. Link would say something to make Carter laugh and give him that dazzling smile, and Carter would forget all about Matthew and his own aching loneliness.

"What is Link's last name?" Paige types on her phone with one hand while the other is getting buffed and polished.

Carter watches her. He's hesitant to admit it, but, "I don't remember."

"Okay... occupation?" Her thumb flies over her phone screen.

"I don't—um. Furniture... artist... sculptor?" He doesn't know how to explain what Link does, exactly, because he doesn't understand it completely himself. Something like that.

Paige's eyes narrow briefly, then she returns to her rapid-fire typing and scrolling. "You could not be more useless if you tried, Carter." She flicks him a sidelong glare. "Forget it, I'll just go through Matthew's profile and find the ex. Or not ex. Or, like, whatever the fuck he's doing. Or *whoever*." She chuckles to herself.

"Paige," Carter starts, knowing the answer, yet hoping he's wrong. "What are you doing?"

"I'm cyberstalking your ex to find his ex to find her ex, duh." She rolls her eyes, then clicks her tongue as she scrolls through whatever she's found. "Wow. If you had done this before, you probably would have seen all this coming. Jamie's been liking Matthew's pictures and tagging him in stuff and commenting on like everything he posts. It's totally blatant."

Carter shakes his head. What does that have to do with anything? His Aunt Diane does the same thing all the time. "So what?"

"So what? It means this has been going on for months, that's what. You dumbass." Paige looks over to her manicurist, Marta, with a look that seems to say, *can you believe him?* The manicurist seems to agree with Paige. "Ooh, found Link. Hello, cheekbones." She squints, scanning Link's "about" page. "They?" she says.

"They." Carter confirms. "Link is nonbinary." He glances over and sees that it's written on Link's profile. Slumped in his seat, hands held uselessly in front of him, he awaits her obnoxious commentary. How long does he have to keep these stupid mittens on? Babette has disappeared. He scowls at his hands.

Would it have mattered if he'd been keeping close tabs on Matthew's social media and realized what was going on months ago? If he's as desperate for love and acceptance as Paige says, then probably not. He'd have ignored it the way he ignored everything else.

Paige tips her head and goes back to her digital stalking. "Mmm-kay."

"No comment on that?" Carter says, needling her, preemptively defensive.

"First of all," she says, "I'm like, super woke. Second of all, who am I to judge how other people live their lives?"

Carter shoots up from his chair. "All you ever do is judge my life!"

Paige switches her phone to her other hand and waves him off with the freshly manicured one. Her fingernails have little jewels on them. "I said people. Not you."

She is *so* irritating. Carter reaches for her phone with his stupid useless mitten hands, and accidentally bats it to the ground. Paige shrieks and dives for it, knocking down nail polish bottles and shallow bowls of wax and water in the process. The manicurist yelps.

"Sorry, sorry," Carter says to Marta, and *not* to Paige, while he tries and fails to help pick up the mess. *Freaking mitten hands.* Paige sits up and shoves Carter into his seat. Her always perfectly wavy hair is a staticky mess from diving under the nail table and her left hand is smeared with pink polish. He feels bad—a little.

"What is your *damage*?" she yells.

Sympathy evaporating as quickly as it came, Carter yells back, "My damage? What is *your* damage? All you have done all morning is criticize me and then stalk my ex and tell me that his leaving me is somehow my fault!" He yanks the mittens off, then peels the paraffin away from his skin. He's trying to look angry and fed up, but the wax is coming off in frustrating, tiny crumbles and he looks like an idiot. "If your mission was to make sure that I won't miss you a single bit after I move to New Orleans tomorrow, well, congratulations, you've succeeded."

He stands to walk off dramatically, but Paige stops him with a hand on his chest. "What did I tell you?" she says to her manicurist. "Drama queen." Marta purses her lips and nods in agreement. "Sit," Paige tells him. He does. She closes her eyes and takes a long breath, as if she's steeling herself to do something very unpleasant, like unclog a toilet. "Carter. Matt leaving was not your fault. And you deserve better than someone who only wants you as his backup plan. Okay? Forget Matthew. He was never good enough for you."

Carter picks at the crumbly paraffin still coating his hands. "Really?"

"Yes. And this Link… you two clearly have a connection, so…" She holds up her phone. Link's profile is pulled up on the screen.

It's as easy as a friend request, maybe a quick message. But if Link wanted that, they would have written something more than Carter's name on that note they'd started at the hotel, or not snuck out while Carter was asleep after that incredible night following one of the best days of Carter's entire life. He looks away from the screen and shakes his head.

"I can't."

"Fine," Paige chirps. "I will."

"Paige, don't," he swipes for the phone again, but she's too fast; she taps something on the screen and then looks at him smugly.

"It's only because I care, little brother." She pats his hand and gives him a smile that does sort of look caring. As awful as she is to him—and she is—besides Link, Paige is the only person who has been there for him since the beginning of this whole disaster and the *only* person who is still there.

"Thanks for caring, I guess," Carter mumbles, frowning at his crumbly palms.

She squeezes his arm, smiles again, and replies, "You know they do earlobe waxing here." She looks deliberately at his ears, then loudly announces that she has to pee and trots off to the bathroom. Carter touches his ears. They aren't hairy. Are they?

Babette finally returns from her leave of absence.

After finally getting the paraffin wax fully removed, Carter waits on the sidewalk. It's covered in slushy, dirty snow. His hands are soft and smooth inside his pockets, and his earlobes sting. After paying, Paige joins him, typing away on her phone. "I just had. The best. Idea."

"If it's surgically embedding your phone into your skull, most people just call that a brain," Carter says, walking to Paige's car.

"Ha ha. Shut up," Paige retorts, but with barely any venom. "No. I'm coming with you!"

Carter narrows his eyes. "Yes, we drove here together in your car because you think my car is, quote, basic."

"All the cars in the world, and you pick a used, tan Toyota Corolla? I—" She stops, adjusts her coat and scarf, and stands taller. "No. I meant to New Orleans. I'm coming with you."

SEVENTEEN

CARTER IS ALL SET: His boss has agreed to let him work remotely while he "deals with a personal issue," though he's left the timeline and details intentionally vague so he can come back if this whole ill-thought-out scheme crashes and burns, as it probably will. He has informed his parents of his plans in a very brief email. He's put his mail on hold, shipped his summer clothes, and boxed up his winter clothes. He has just enough essentials secured in the trunk of his car to get him started in a new place, he's removed his name from all utilities and the lease for his old condo, and he's told Paige approximately eight hundred times that she is not coming with him to New Orleans, no way, no how, not ever. No.

"You don't own New Orleans; you don't get to say who can and can't go there." Paige follows him as he brings a final load of laundry into her living room to be folded and packed.

He ignores her; they've had this argument. He'll explain that he's moving in order to get rid of his baggage, not bring it with him, and she'll get offended at being called baggage, and then he'll have to explain all the ways in which she's dragging him down and ruining his life, like baggage. But he's on a strict schedule, he just doesn't have the time.

"If I come, you won't be alone," Paige says, trying a different tactic, but not one she hasn't already tried. And he's already told her that he needs to be alone, that's part of the point. Part of what Stan the security guard—and Paige herself—helped him see is that he doesn't even know what he wants, he just knows he needs time to figure it out—alone.

"I heard back from Link," Paige says. Carter pauses his folding and packing. He's thought about contacting Link so many times; Link would get it, why he's doing this. And he's also desperate to know how Link is doing. Has Jamie come back, the way Matthew did? Is Link happy? Does Link ever think of Carter?

Carter drops a pile of clothes into his suitcase. "It doesn't matter now."

Paige crosses her arms, then sits on top of his suitcase. "Well, I'm coming with you, and you can't stop me."

So mature. "Look, I know you're gonna miss me." Carter grunts as he tries to push Paige off his suitcase. "But maybe this will be a good time for you to focus on dating, finding someone special, and making them miserable instead of me. Get. Off."

There's a brief scuffle, and some yelling, a little cursing, and then both Paige and his suitcase fall to the floor. Carter has to repack *everything*. He is now officially behind schedule. "I thought you'd be happy to see me go, Paige. What is this?" Carter tosses clothes back into his suitcase while Paige sulks nearby.

She mumbles something.

"Sorry? I didn't catch that." *Ugh*, all his clothes will get wrinkled, and he left the iron back at the condo.

"I said," Paige starts. She uncrosses her arms and fixes a few flyaway hairs. "I lost my job."

"Oh." Carter closes his suitcase; that's gonna have to be good enough. "That's too bad."

"It is, and, like, I was depressed so I bought some shoes to cheer me up, but it didn't work. So I bought some more shoes." She chews at the end of her thumb and looks at her feet. "Then I sort of lost control and spent all of my money and couldn't make rent so they're evicting me and I don't have anywhere else to go. I had to put our manicures on four different credit cards. I'm the pathetic, desperate one. *Me*." She slumps onto the sofa, once again knocking his suitcase to the floor.

She looks sad. Actually, really, for real sad.

Carter sighs, looks up, and rubs his palms over his face. "Dammit."

*   *   *

THEY HAVEN'T EVEN CROSSED THE Illinois state line before Carter is ready to drop Paige off at the next rest area. First, she had a loud, hour-long phone conversation with someone—whom, Carter never figured out—in which her contribution to the discussion was mostly sudden exclamations of "No way!" and "Shut up!" Then she took her shoes off and put her bare feet up on the immaculate dash of Carter's Toyota. And now she's flipping through music stations while texting: talk radio, pop, country, commercial, commercial, religious talk radio, country, rock, rap, polka, alternative, jazz, classical, R&B, political talk radio.

"Can you just *pick* something?" Carter snaps; his fingers clench on the steering wheel.

"Wow, jeez." Paige widens her eyes at him, pretending to be innocent. "Okay, fine, here you go."

They listen to an '80s hair-metal station until the signal fades. Carter's jaw clenches to match his hands. They cross the border into Missouri as the morning sun rises high, then make a stop just past St. Louis so Carter can get some coffee and gas up the car; he hates going below half a tank. Paige goes inside to use the restroom and get a snack while Carter pumps gas, and she still isn't finished when he buys his weak, too-hot coffee, still isn't finished when he buckles up and puts the key in the ignition. She'd probably be fine in St. Louis. Paige is adaptable, makes friends easily. And she has her cell phone with her, so—

"What are you staring off into space about?" Paige drops into the passenger seat with a can of Pringles tucked under one arm. "Do you need a nap? 'Cause I can drive."

Carter starts the engine. "Like hell you're driving my car." Paige is a distracted driver of the worst kind with her cell phone glued to her ear and her mind everywhere but on the road. He'd like to make it to New Orleans alive and preferably not maimed. Planning ahead this time, Carter plays NPR through the app on his phone and lets a story about an electric carmaker in China settle the tension in his shoulders.

The traffic is light on this stretch of 55, and Paige is on a quiet social media binge while she scarfs down Pringles.

Too anxious about the move and the drive, Carter barely ate before they left in the pre-dawn darkness. "Can I have a chip?" Carter reaches for the can. Paige moves it out of his reach and slaps his hand.

"This can of Pringles is the last purchase I made with the last two dollars left in my account, Carter. These Pringles are the most important thing in my life now. I can't believe you would try to take that from me."

Carter rolls his eyes so hard he accidentally drifts to the left lane. "Sorry I asked," he says, as he settles back into the right lane at a reasonable four miles over the speed limit. He may be imagining it, but he swears Paige crunches her next chip extra loud to rub it in.

The drive will take them through Arkansas, over briefly through the westernmost end of Tennessee, and then cover a very long stretch of Mississippi. Carter engages the cruise control and stretches his ankle a bit while the road is clear. Something bumps his arm.

"Hey!" He flinches, then, "Oh." Paige offers him the rest of the Pringles. There are only four left, but still. "Thanks," he says, sincerely. They are the most important thing in the world to her, after all.

After a long, quiet stretch of highway, Paige tosses her phone aside, groans, and announces, "God, this is *so boring*." Before Carter can remind her, yet again, that she did not have to come along and is free to go away at any time, she demands, "So other than Matt, what are you running from?"

EIGHTEEN

"I'M NOT RUNNING FROM ANYTHING," Carter says after another long stretch of road. Though he did quite literally run away from Matthew at the condo, he'd like to think he's running *toward* something.

"It's totally understandable," Paige says, putting her feet back up on the dashboard. "I'd be too humiliated to stay in Aurora too."

"Gee, thanks, Paige."

She shrugs. "Just keeping it real."

Nobody ever asks you to, Carter thinks. He grits his teeth instead of saying it. In truth, he hasn't thought a whole lot about why he's moving and why so quickly. He needs a fresh start, sure, and he needs to sort out what to do with his life, but he's typically not so hasty about, well, anything. He's been stuck, and it took everything falling apart to propel him forward. New Orleans seems like as a good a place as any to get unstuck. Even now when he thinks of his time there, his chest warms and his mouth tips into a helpless smile. How much of that has to do with the city and how much with Link is a path he can't travel right now.

"I'm going because…" Though he doesn't owe Paige an explanation and isn't interested in her judgment, he also doesn't want this new chapter of his life to be tied up with Matthew in any way, because it isn't. "Back in Aurora, every direction I looked in felt like a dead end. In New Orleans, at least, I have possibilities. At least I'm excited about what *might* be."

Paige is looking at her phone, typing something and not even paying attention to what he said in response to *her* question. Carter shakes his head and focuses on the road. After a while, they enter Mississippi, where the highway stretches on and on, interminably.

"That's why I'm going too," Paige says. At first, Carter isn't sure it's directed at him, as she's still staring at her phone screen. "I hated that job, you know." He didn't know. He hasn't exactly been paying close attention to Paige's life. "And like," she continues, "I was never gonna quit because the pay was awesome and the perks were even better but—*ugh*. You know?"

He doesn't. He nods anyway. "Sure."

"So even though I was *way* depressed at first, now I think it's for the best." She stretches her legs out on top of the dashboard until her toes reach the windshield and leave little toe marks. *Ugh*, indeed. "I like that: What might be. I forget that you're smart sometimes, Carter."

"That's very charitable of you, Paige." Carter replies. "Now please get your disgusting feet off my windshield, or I am leaving you in Mississippi."

At a rest area in Kentwood, Louisiana, it's warm enough for Carter to shed his cardigan. He takes a moment in the grass outside of the restroom to stretch his spine, shake the numbness from his legs, and turn his face to the sun. *Running toward something.* He's been grudging about Paige's intentions, perhaps, assuming she just wanted to bother him and get a free vacation, which she is. But he never would have expected that she'd been stuck, too, or that she'd been unhappy. It's always been Paige who has the easier time; she's popular, outgoing, likable, *normal* in ways Carter never managed to be. Yet being those things doesn't preclude the sort of unhappiness that forces one to desperately pretend to be anything but. Matthew is living proof of that.

Carter approaches the car where Paige is sitting on the hood, on her phone. He's so excited, he doesn't even care that she's scuffing the paint. "All right, next stop: New Orleans!"

Paige snaps her fingers. "Let me drive. At your grandpa pace we'll never get there." She looks up, hand held out expectantly for the keys, and gives him a look of disdain. "Have you been wearing that shirt this whole time? Carter."

He plucks at his red, blue, and green gingham oxford. "What's wrong with my shirt?"

"I don't even have time to start with that." She snaps her fingers again. "Keys."

Carter tosses her the keys, rolling his eyes at her as he does so. On second thought, he's probably been *too* charitable toward Paige. With any luck, she'll hate New Orleans and go home soon, and finally, finally Carter can start over.

Onward.

It's dark again by the time they arrive in the city and Carter gets everything signed and approved and has his house keys in hand.

"Well, this place is a dump," Paige announces as they walk up the cracked driveway.

"Takes one to know one," Carter quips, and walks up the porch steps to his brand-new home without waiting for a response. The house's windows are boarded up. The doorknob nearly comes off in his hand, and he's immediately met with the smell of moldy carpet and the sight of peeling wallpaper and flaking, stained popcorn ceilings. It's perfect. "This is known as a 'camelback' style," Carter says, taking in the high ceilings of the living room. "It's a variation of the popular shotgun style—which some believe is so-named because you could shoot a single shot from the front of the house and it would go straight through to the end without touching a single wall." He pretends to shoot a gun. "The camelback has a small second floor that would have been attached to the rear at a later date, adding more living space to homes at a time when taxation was based on lot frontage."

"Wow," Paige says from behind him. "That is super boring."

"It's simple, sturdy, and lends itself to any number of architectural styles," Carter continues, heedless of Paige's disinterest. "This one is Italianate, my personal favorite. Note the decorative entablature and parapet over the front porch that are supported by Doric columns and decorative quoins."

"Boy, did I," Paige says, probably sarcastically.

"This one was built in 1909, probably one of the last of its style, and still completely un-refurbished." It's even better than the pictures he's been poring over. He'd been worried about buying it sight unseen, but it's exactly as he'd hoped.

"It looks like the carpet hasn't been cleaned since 1909," Paige says, kicking at a huge stain with the toe of her shoe. It's all coming out; it doesn't matter how dirty it is. The wallpaper and popcorn ceilings are going too. Paige looks around with clear distaste. "So this is where we're staying."

Carter laughs. "Uh, no, *we* are not staying anywhere. I am staying here, in my house, which is mine."

Paige swings around to face him so fast that her monogrammed duffel bag swings out and collides with his hip. "Like I want to stay in your gross house anyway."

"Don't let the door hit you on the way out, then." Carter walks into the kitchen to take stock of what will need to be torn out. "Or, actually: *Do* let the door hit you."

Due to the style and size of the house, Paige can stand at the front door while Carter is in the very back room, and, locked in a tense standoff, they can glare at each other through the kitchen in between. Paige relents first, crosses her arms petulantly, and asks, "How many bedrooms upstairs?"

"Two," Carter says, peering up the narrow staircase. "Pick whichever one you want; they're the same size."

The house has been stripped of appliances, the cabinets are in rough shape, and he's brought no furniture. Everything will be a project. They have no beds to sleep in. He's so excited. Paige creaks up the steps and, from the sounds of the groaning floorboards, seems to settle in the bedroom on the left. Carter hefts his suitcase onto the kitchen counter and pulls out a carefully wrapped package.

There's a mantel in the living room, but no fireplace, just drywall-patched spots on the wall beneath and the ceiling above where a woodstove must have been. Carter unwraps the birdhouse Link gave him and places it gently on the mantel. Now he really does have the historic New Orleans home he's always wanted. Now he can finally move on, baggage-free. Paige yells for him from upstairs, and Carter sighs. Almost baggage-free.

NINETEEN

ONE NIGHT ON A LEAKY air mattress that was hastily procured from a nearby drugstore after Paige won rock-paper-scissors for the nice one he brought was one night too many, so early the next morning Carter tells Paige to be useful and sends her off to a camping store for a sleeping bag and floor pad. He doesn't want to get furniture or appliances or anything permanent until he's pulled up the carpet and seen what he's working with underneath. Carter takes his laptop and goes to a nearby city park to work on digital floor plan renderings.

The house is right in the heart of the city, on the outskirts of a neighborhood filled with classic, historic New Orleans homes. Some have been overhauled and updated with shiny new finishes and spotless landscaping, and some—like his—are in various states of decay and disrepair. His walk takes him past a block of restaurants and bars that are lively with music and conversation, on to a worn-out baseball field behind a rusted fence, then past a mural painted across a cement wall and an empty lot overgrown with weeds.

Beautifully refurbished houses sit right next to others that are crumbling on their foundations, which sit next to modestly maintained family homes. He passes an old church, a new gas station, the trolley line, and a busy four-lane intersection. One of those creepy city-of-the-dead cemeteries comes into view on his right; a modern art museum is on his left. It's less shiny than the New Orleans he experienced with Link, now that he's in a part of town where people live and work: no street parties, no glitz, no tour guides, no room service breakfast and daily fresh beignets.

At the park, Carter settles on a bench that looks out over a small lake. The faint sounds of traffic are behind him. The farthest he'd lived away from Aurora was the small private college he attended in Naperville, roughly twenty miles from the house he grew up in. The house he shared with roommates during grad school was twelve miles away from his childhood home. The condo he shared with Matthew was ten. Perhaps, then, this feeling of being out of place, unanchored, and filled with increasing, panicked regret is normal, and he's just never experienced it before.

Carter opens his laptop to work on a modern, traditional two-story home with an open floor plan and a mix of farmhouse and Greco-Roman design: rustic and homey, yet stately and ornate, a series of contradictions he's long since grown used to. Carter can create this sort of plan in his sleep, but today he can't seem to focus.

He opens a second tab with a blank blueprint draft for his own home. It sits there, untouched, waiting for his decisions. But aside from pulling out the carpet and the wall coverings that are hiding the original elements of the home, he doesn't know what he wants to do with it. He has spent so long making plans for other people, he doesn't know how to move forward for himself. Panic bubbles up, catching in his chest. What if this is all a terrible mistake? He's uprooted his entire life, bought a derelict home in a city he's only spent one week in—a week entirely removed from reality at that—and all on the sketchy advice of a stoned security guard.

This is all a terrible mistake.

And Matthew, Matthew offered him a chance to talk. What if *he's* also made a terrible mistake? This whole thing could have been a bump in the road, cold feet about getting married. His parent's marriage is riddled with bumps, and they're still hanging in there. Not happily, but he can't expect a relationship to be easy all the time. He and Matthew have their problems, but doesn't everyone? Is he no worse than Matthew for leaving as he did?

Carter closes his eyes and groans. Paige is right; he is going to go crawling back. He is that weak. A small flock of mallards drifts by. Carter watches them until they're all the way across the lake, then opens his laptop again and clicks a third tab. He's never social media-stalked anyone before, but it's easy enough: From his own profile page he finds his list of "friends" and clicks on Paige's name. He's immediately assaulted with photo after photo of Paige and her girls, and Paige and her shopping, and Paige and *her girls* shopping. He goes to Paige's friend list and discovers Matthew's name listed first. Right under it is Link's. Link Boudreaux, whose profile picture is a close-up of the left side of their face. Their full lips are quirked just a little, hazel-gold eyes downcast. Barely visible in the background is a quote, spray-painted in purple on a white wall: *"Art is anything you can get away with."*

The panic in Carter's chest dissipates, replaced by a buzzing warmth. He wishes that he and Link had had more than a week, yet right now he's grateful they had anything at all. Deciding to quit while he's ahead, Carter closes the tab and finally gets some work done. He'll leave the digital stalking to Paige.

As soon as he gets home, Paige accosts him with a *Price is Right* style showcase of everything she bought. "So I got two sleeping pads, two sleeping bags, two solar-powered lamps and two high-end camping chairs."

Carter surveys the pile of camping gear in his living room. "One sleeping bag and one mat, Paige. That's all I asked you to get." He should have known better; Paige takes shopping more seriously than she took her job. "How did you even afford all of this with what I gave you to spend?"

Paige claps, bouncing up and down. "That's the best part! It was all on sale *and* part of a bundle. Plus!" She scurries into the room that may become a formal dining room and comes back with even more stuff. "*Plus*, I joined their VIP program and got forty percent off my next purchase, so I went back and got this camping stove and cook set." She sets them both on the counter. "And then I signed up for a store credit card and got this cool knife." She pulls a knife from her pocket and flicks it open.

Carter instinctively cowers away and covers his heart, horrified.

Paige flicks the utility knife closed again. "Relax. If I wanted to kill you I would have smothered you last night when you were snoring. Stabbing you would be too messy."

Carter relaxes from his protective stance. "Paige, this is…" He considers the stuff, and how much he did need all of it. "Actually, it's pretty great."

"Really?" She looks up at him with a surprised smile.

"Yeah, I—I'm…" He can't believe he's saying this. "Glad that you're here."

"Aw," Paige says. "Well, I'm glad I didn't smother you in your sleep, then."

It's as close to a bonding moment as they're going to get, so Carter nods and turns to choose a sleeping bag and foam pad. He wants to tear out the wood paneling in the upstairs rooms today, and they should have time to get some shelf-stable groceries before dinnertime. It will be really nice to cook something at home and not eat out for the first time in weeks. She did it in her usual bullheaded way—disregarding his wishes and doing whatever the hell she wants—but, thanks to Paige, he does feel a bit more settled.

Carter arranges his little bed in a corner of the right hand room upstairs, then scans the walls for the loosest corner to start yanking out the wood panels. Usually he'd need a pry bar, but the paneling is so old and warped that it pulls right off.

"Hey, Carter." Paige pops in and watches, but does not offer to help.

"Yeah?" Carter says impatiently, distracted by the splinters he keeps getting. Tomorrow he's finding a hardware store and getting tools and gloves.

"Just to make sure: You two haven't been in contact, right?"

Carter winces, pulling another splinter from his palm. "Like I said, Link made it pretty clear that we were only temporary. I'm being respectful of that." It's why he didn't click that friend-request button or keep trying to find more information on Link and how they're doing, no matter how much he may want to.

Paige hums. "I was actually talking about Matthew. Curious."

"Why is that curious?" he calls to Paige's retreating back. She says nothing. "Paige!" Carter sets his hands on his hips and stares at the empty door, then shrugs it off. She's clearly just trying to get to him. After a few more splinters and some cursing, Carter finally pulls a panel free, then immediately wishes he hadn't.

TWENTY

"I'm going shopping," Carter says, first thing when Paige gets out of bed. After a night bunking in her room due to the spider colony he unearthed behind the wood paneling in his bedroom, Carter makes fresh coffee on the little camping stove and decides he won't shake Paige off and go by himself. He's feeling generous toward her this morning. "We can take the trolley up to the French Quarter; there's a café with these pastries you have to try. And then we'll walk to the Saturday Art Market."

Paige squints at him. "You're being sweet, and it's weird."

He slept comfortably last night. It's been some time since that's happened, and he got the shower working this morning after a run to the hardware store. He'd pushed all of his worries and misgivings into getting that showerhead on securely. He feels *great*.

"I'm sweet all the time, just not with you."

Paige sips her coffee and comments, "I don't think I'm a fan of it."

The exterminators arrive. Carter shows them to the spider-wall and doesn't even want to consider that there are probably more of them still hidden away.

"Stay if you want to, then." Carter puts on shoes and grabs his wallet. It's a perfect spring morning; he doesn't even need a coat.

Paige nods toward the upstairs, clearly still deciding whether or not she wants to hang out with him. "Isn't that stuff pretty poisonous, though? Those guys were in, like, full-on hazmat suits."

Carter opens the door and smiles. "We can only hope."

The house is a long way away from needing any interior design elements, but Carter is hoping the art market he read about on a flyer at the hardware store will jump-start his inspiration. He may not be artistic, but all that creativity in one place has to kick-start *something*. On the way, Paige complains: about the walk, the sun, the pace Carter is setting—too fast, then too slow. Carter is regretting not leaving her behind to be engulfed in bug spray, when their mother calls him. Paige plucks the phone from his hand and answers. Carter stands in line for beignets while Paige distracts her with gossip about a cousin's rumored infidelity.

"Thanks," Carter says, handing her the warm, sugar-dusted paper bag and taking his phone back with the call finished.

"We better be done walking," Paige responds. "Or I'm taking a cab. By myself."

"Just a little farther."

When they finally make it, Paige ducks into a bathroom to touch up her makeup and "blow dry her pits." Carter wanders the nearby stalls. It's like a flea market, but all the wares are handmade. He peruses jewelry and paintings and artsy photographs and nearly buys a set of ceramic coffee cups with a matching pot, but he doesn't really have anywhere to put it, so he walks away. Carter can't yet visualize what the house might look like when he's finished. He's a detail person; he's always left the big picture stuff to other people. He does get in a long line to buy a bag of roasted nuts.

"Carter?"

Paige must be finished and looking for him. But it doesn't sound like Paige. It sounds like—Carter spins around, coming face-to-face with a tall metal sculpture that looks like a plant from the bottom of the ocean: gothic and eerie and beautiful. And behind that—

"Carter Jacob?"

He has to blink several times, opening and closing his mouth without making a sound. He can't possibly be seeing what he's seeing.

"Link?"

At a booth filled with more metal sculptures and metal furniture, with blown glass art pieces lining a back shelf, stands Link. Carter's breath rasps; the ground beneath him shifts. He wishes he hadn't let Paige eat all the beignets and that he had consumed something more substantial than coffee before walking all the way here. He stumbles woozily, listing forward and catching himself on the deep-sea-plant sculpture. It does not hold his weight, and with it, Carter goes tumbling into the dirt.

He hears his name, tries to get his feet under him, and then a gentle, steady hand tugs him up to sit. It's Link, crouching and touching his face and looking at him with such care and concern that Carter sways again.

"This might be a silly question, but are you okay?"

Despite his shock and subsequent humiliation, Carter is too woozy to fight his awe at running into Link. "Yeah. I'm okay now."

Link insists on settling Carter behind the booth in a metal chair, then rushes off to get him food and something to drink. Carter inspects himself, so surprised at seeing Link that he didn't even take note of the scrape on his elbow and the way his hip hit the sharp metal sculpture. He rubs at it, and Link returns with crêpes in a Styrofoam box and a huge plastic cup of lemonade, then tuts over Carter's injuries.

"I can't believe you're here."

"Me either," Carter says, meaning both of them. Sitting on the table in front of him is a metal scorpion made of nuts, bolts, and wrenches. Carter feels better after eating, promises that he's not hurt, not really, and apologizes for taking out a one of kind art piece and scaring Link half to death. Link swears it's fine, no big, and then the realization of the last time they were together, what they did, how Link left, seems to hit them both at the same time.

"I should go," Carter says

"Carter, I wanted to—" Link starts, talking over him.

They both go quiet.

"Link, you wanna go grab something? Oh, you got crêpes…" A cute redhead with several tattoos and a lip piercing approaches the booth, slows at seeing Carter, then steps behind the display table to join them. "Is everything okay?"

Carter stands. "I have to find my sister, so." As if he conjured her, Paige appears around the corner and spots him. She's clearly annoyed at how far he wandered.

"Um, how sweaty did you think my armpits were? Oh, hello. I'm Paige."

Link nods in apparent recognition. "Paige? *Paige.* Okay, things are starting to make sense now. Hi, I'm Link. Nice to officially meet you." Paige and Link shake hands, then Link turns to introduce the redhead. "This is Eli. We share a studio space and collaborate sometimes. His stuff is the blown glass."

Paige reaches for Eli's hand and bats her eyelashes. "Well, hello there." She and Eli shake hands far longer than necessary. Paige twirls a strand of hair with her other hand. Carter is going to vomit up his crêpe. He clears his throat until they cut it out.

"What brings you to New Orleans?" Eli asks, looking at Paige.

"Oh, I'm just in town to help Carter get settled."

Link turns to Carter this time. "Settled?"

Carter shifts awkwardly away. People wander by the booth, and a band plays in the distance. Of all the ways he wanted to talk to Link, to see them again, at a public market after he nearly passed out—while his sister makes bedroom eyes at a cute stranger—was not anywhere close. Link looks incredible, too. Carter has to move to the other side of the booth and put the table between him and Link before he can speak. "I moved here, yeah. Just needed a change, and when I was here I guess I fell in love."

Link's mouth parts with surprise.

"With the city!" Carter rushes to say. "I fell in love with New Orleans. The city. The city of New Orleans." Paige shoots him a *what the hell is wrong with you* look. "So, anyways. Yeah," Carter finishes, frowning at his own awkwardness.

"Wow. Carter, that's—good for you." Links finally says after another very awkward pause. "It is a pretty amazing place; I can't really blame you."

"What are you—" Carter reaches across the table, realizes what he's doing, drops his hand to the scorpion, and pets it, awkwardly. "What are you doing back here in New Orleans?"

Link frowns. "Carter, I live here. I thought you knew that?"

It takes a minute, but the puzzle pieces slot into place. Carter is the biggest idiot in the entire world. Of course: Link navigated the city like the back of their hand, had insider info about things to do, talked about partly growing up here. Has an accent reminiscent of New Orleans natives. Has Creole and Cajun roots and is *working* at a booth in New Orleans at this *very moment.*

"Right," Carter says.

"I thought that was like, the whole point of this," Paige cuts in, exasperated. "You seriously suck at stalking people, Carter."

Link blushes, Carter glares, and Eli laughs. "So, Carter. *The* Carter. I've heard a lot about you." Eli reaches for Carter's hand and gives it a brisk shake.

Link has talked about him. A lot.

"Good things, I hope, since I've made a pretty bad impression today," Carter says, attempting a joke to lighten the uncomfortable mood.

Eli tilts his head and lifts an eyebrow. "Well. Things," he says. Link jabs an elbow into Eli's ribs. "That I am keeping to myself."

Carter's stomach squirms; he's made such a huge mess of everything. Has he always been this dense? Judging by Paige's long-suffering expression, he guesses so.

"I, uh. I should go."

Carter leaves, not waiting for a response or for Paige to follow. Link lives here, and Carter had to have known that. Somewhere in his muddled brain and his bruised heart, he *knew.*

TWENTY-ONE

IT'S ONLY DUE TO PAIGE'S intervention that Carter doesn't immediately get in his car and drive back to Aurora. She tells him to sleep on it, and that tomorrow he should get in touch with Link and have an honest conversation. Instead, Carter of thinks of nothing but the house, of ripping up, tearing down, breaking apart. Paige remains, day after day, keeping herself busy and away, doing what, Carter doesn't know and doesn't care. He spends every spare moment on demolition, going to bed every night sore and exhausted and falling immediately into a dreamless sleep. He doesn't intend to stop until the house has been stripped to its bones.

"Eli invited us over to watch a basketball game tonight." Paige leans against the doorframe of the upstairs bathroom where Carter is busy and has told her that repeatedly. She looks overdressed for watching a basketball game, as if she's going on a date. Carter's fingers ache from hours of pulling moldy grout out from between the bathtub tiles; his knees ache from kneeling in the bathtub for so long. He doesn't move, and he doesn't stop pulling out the thin lines of grout.

"Link will be there," Paige says.

Carter pauses, briefly, then continues his work. The tiles are probably the original ones in this shower, though not from when the house was built at the turn of the century, of course, because it wouldn't have had an indoor bathroom. "The tiles in here look to be mid-century," Carter says, to say something; his brain seizes on the only thing that makes sense to him right now. It's cobalt blue, the tile; its polish has dulled over time. "Once I get new grout in and do a deep clean to get rid of all the mineral deposits and soap scum it'll really be something."

"Okay, Bob Vila," Paige says. "Time to leave the house."

Carter is surprised that she knows who Bob Vila is. He shakes his head. "I'm fine."

"No," Paige says, wrenching the grout saw from his claw-like hand. "You're emotionally constipated. That's not the same thing as being fine."

"I am not…" He's crouched in the tub for so long that his leg muscles have almost begun to atrophy, and his attempt to grab the tool back ends with him falling onto his ass in the tub. "…emotionally constipated," he finishes, feebly rubbing at his knees and numb legs. "I just really want to get this place livable."

Paige perches on the counter, careful to avoid the spot where the base of the faucet is cracked and water leaks out, warping the old blue laminate countertops. Those need to go too. "Okay, all you've done is take stuff down. You've spent all day today sitting in the freaking bathtub just chiseling out little bits of caulk."

"Grout." Carter sounds robotic as he says, "Grout is porous and used to fill in spaces between tiles. Caulk is nonporous and used as a sealant on the seams and corners."

"Oh my *god*, Carter. I don't care." The bit of tentative gentleness she had in her voice earlier is gone. "The point is, you've holed yourself up in this dump, made it look like even more of a dump, and you haven't even put in a refrigerator! We're still camping out on sleeping bags and making ramen noodles on a hot plate for dinner like barbarians!"

Carter drops his head back on the edge of the bathtub. Why is she still here then, why does she care? She has a life waiting for her back home, friends, dates, *options*. He has this house and nothing else. He's too tired to argue with her, so he stares up at the yellow water stain on the ceiling—the roof will need to be fixed as well—and mumbles, "I want to make sure everything is right before I start rebuilding. It's called being thorough."

"No, it's called you being so fucked up because of Matthew that you're terrified to commit to anything and so embarrassed by what happened with Link that you're hiding." Paige hops down from the counter. "Enough."

Carter scowls, turning away to curl in the tub. "Way to kick me when I'm down. Thanks for that, Paige."

"Oh, Carter," Paige says with a sigh. "Stop being so difficult."

"Ah, yes." Carter gives a quick, rueful laugh. "*Stop being so difficult, Carter*, a Jacob family classic." Paige tries to rephrase, but Carter waves her off. "Just go without me. No one wants me there anyway."

Paige sighs. Her feet thunk back onto the floor, which creaks as she walks out. Alone again, Carter remains curled in the tub with pins and needles in his legs and hands, waiting for his strength to return so he can get back to the grout removal. Maybe he is hiding, and maybe he *is* afraid to commit to anything, but shouldn't he be? He came all this way to be something else, and he's brought all his issues along with him. If Matthew really will take him back, then at least he won't be so pathetically lonely.

Carter screams and flails as a sudden blast of cold water soaks him from the waist down. Paige is looming menacingly over him, pointing the stream of freezing water from the shower nozzle right at him. "Get out of the tub, or it's your face next."

ELI LIVES IN A NEWER apartment building overlooking downtown. It's small, but well laid-out with an urban-industrial feel: stainless steel appliances, concrete countertops, slate floors, high ceilings with exposed steel beams. Yet it still looks like an artist's home, with funky art pieces and pops of color everywhere, and Eli's glasswork is set here and there.

Carter puts on a pleasant face, exchanges niceties and accepts a glass of wine, and doesn't mention to Eli that he only came under threat of waterboarding because that seems impolite. Eli and Paige fall into easy conversation, leaning close, smiling, touching each other's arms and hands as if this is something they've done many times before. Carter retreats to a corner and leaves them to it. Is this where Paige has been spending her time? With Eli?

He doesn't seem like her usual type: the interchangeable, straight cis dude-bros named Chad or Brad or Brent or Trent. Not that he cares who Paige dates, or that she's ever cared about his opinion one way or the other, but Carter has hated every guy she's dated and introduced him to. Eli, though—scruffy, laid-back, tattooed and pierced, artist Eli—seems okay. He friended Carter on Facebook, Twitter, and Instagram right away, even though Carter doesn't use any of them much. Watching Paige happily cuddle next to someone on the couch while Carter is still trying to sweep the dusty pieces of his heart off the floor again, though, seems both terribly unfair and exactly what he should have expected.

The basketball game starts, and the dozen or so people who were scattered around the apartment all find a spot around the TV. Carter spots Link hanging out in the back of the room, watching the game and chatting with a few people, dressed in a red and blue basketball jersey and matching red skinny jeans, with a sweep of blue eyeliner and glossy pink lips. Their hair is loose and shining, and they are as beautiful as ever, maybe more so.

Carter stays put in his corner. He misses the bathtub. No one would notice if he left right now. Hardly anyone has even noticed he's here. Link looks over, smiles, waves, then turns away. Carter will quickly take in the view from the balcony before he leaves; that will be a reasonably considerate length of time to stay.

From the balcony, the view of New Orleans is of a modern skyline with sleek new buildings. It's a city of such complexity and seeming contradictions, a city in flux. Carter thought he could be someone different here, but he keeps making the same mistakes wherever he goes.

"Nice night, huh?" Eli steps out of the sliding glass door and closes it behind him.

"Sure," Carter says.

Eli leans over the railing next to him. A small blown-glass pipe is cradled in one hand, a lighter in the other. He sparks a green bud nestled inside the pipe, and pungent, earthy-sweet smoke drifts over to Carter. Eli holds the pipe out.

"No, thanks." Carter holds up a hand. "I'm very impulsive when I'm stoned." Apparently. That and Stan are what got him into this mess.

"Is that bad thing?" Eli asks after taking another drag.

For him? "Yes."

Eli lifts his chin, takes another puff, then snuffs the cherry out with the plastic end of his lighter. "I don't partake often. Pelicans games stress me out, though."

Carter nods and says, "I hear that," even though he hadn't even known New Orleans had a basketball team until an hour ago and certainly not that they were called *Pelicans.* The quiet settles uncomfortably between them. Carter shifts from side to side, looking toward the front door. It would be impolite to leave now. It's impolite to stand here and say nothing.

"You make that?" Carter says, conversationally, nodding at the glass pipe.

"Yep," Eli replies. "Some of my best sellers."

"Nice."

"Yeah. Thanks."

After another awkward silence Carter adds, "So, you and Paige?"

Eli tips his head to hide a shy smile. "I guess yeah. We've been hanging out. Are you gonna give me the 'don't hurt my sister or I'll hurt you' warning?"

Carter snorts. "No. If anything, you should be worried about *Paige* hurting *you.*" Eli laughs, Carter doesn't.

"Well, I'm pretty tough. Don't worry about me." Eli's expression seems to harden, a lightning quick shift in his so far happy-go-lucky demeanor. He glances inside, where Paige is screaming at the TV, and his face softens further. "I like that she's… very honest. It means I can be honest. We know what we're getting into and how we feel, right away, no hiding. Makes things easier."

It's a concept Carter is unable to relate to. "Right," he says.

Eli rubs at his scruffy chin, picks his hat up, and turns it backward. He seems to be working up to saying something in particular. "You know, I moved out here right after I transitioned. I wanted a fresh start, I guess. I didn't really know just how lonely I'd be. I thought about giving up and going home every day for months even though it wasn't a healthy place for me to be."

Carter looks away. Paige has been talking about him to Eli. Of course she has. He doesn't know what Eli's angle is here, other than to butter Carter up in order to get close to his sister, or do her bidding more likely, but it's not necessary. He and Paige don't have that kind of relationship. "You don't need to worry about me, either," Carter says.

A plane flies overhead, and they watch as its lights blink a path across the night sky. Inside, everyone cheers; something happened in the game that makes Eli glance back. Carter wishes he would just go, as he clearly wants to, so Carter can slip out unnoticed. He is trying though, for whatever reason, so Carter can try a little, too, he guesses.

"When did you start to feel like you should be here?" Carter asks. "Because I am securely in the regretting-it-every-day stage."

Eli's eyelids are heavy, and it takes a second for him to drift out of whatever daydream he was zoned out on. "Hmm. It was gradual. Sold some art. Met Link. Sold some more art. Met some more people. Found a community and a life and… it took a while. Starting over is fucking hard." His nose wrinkles. "Does it sound totally dumb if I say I had to find myself before I could find other people?"

Carter looks over the top of his head and says, unconvincingly. "No…"

Eli laughs. "Well, it's true. Put that shit on a motivational poster."

Carter's mouth twitches. "Over a picture of the beach at sunset."

"Exactly, yes." Eli pushes off from the railing and scoops up the glass pipe and lighter on his way toward the door. "I get it. Link's thing with you."

He slips back inside before Carter can clarify what he means by "thing" and if it's good or bad. Why didn't he get stoned? What would stoned Carter do? If he were more like Paige, he would be honest with Link and tell them that he hasn't gone a single day without wondering how Link is—without missing them—and that he is incredibly confused about where he stands.

He just told himself to be more like Paige. Is this rock bottom?

He and Link catch each other's eyes across the room. Carter panics, bolts for the door and speed-walks down the corridor outside. Well, at least he knows now that stoned Carter and sober Carter both have the same instincts when it comes to flight or fight. Flight wins every time.

TWENTY-TWO

CARTER WAITS FOR THE ELEVATOR to arrive on the tenth floor with his arms crossed and fingers tapping his elbows impatiently. *This is stupid.* He's being stupid. He can occupy the same space as Link without making such a thing of it, or at least he can with the buffer of a group of people and a basketball game to get in between. And wine. Wine helps. If Paige and Eli are whatever they are, it's likely he and Link will run into each other again *if* Carter does stay in New Orleans, and he'll have to figure out a way to be around Link without being so weird.

The elevator arrives; Carter steps forward, then back, then forward again. He groans at himself and turns around. The elevator door closes behind him. Carter runs right into someone.

"Oh, sorry—oh." Carter stumbles back, flushing with embarrassment.

"Hi," Link says.

"Hey. Hi." Carter flattens his hair and spins back to face the closed elevator door. He whistles for some reason. He stares so hard at the shiny metal door he could bore holes through it. In his peripheral vision, he can see Link swaying slightly back and forth, staring up at the ceiling. Finally, there's a ding, and the doors slide open, and, naturally, no one else is inside. Carter steps on and turns to face front. Link does the same, on the far side of the elevator. Carter catches a whiff of coconut; it tugs at his belly. He takes a breath. "You leaving?"

"Mm. Yep. I am," Link says. "You?"

Carter nods. "Yeah."

They're saved from the next stretch of uncomfortable silence when the elevator stops on the ninth floor to pick up a person who is mid-phone conversation and stands between the two of them while talking loudly to someone.

"Yeah, I'm getting off now," the new elevator occupant says. "Well, I very much look forward to meeting your poodle." They step off. The doors close. Link and Carter make eye contact across the elevator and snicker at the same time. The moment doesn't resolve the tension completely, but Carter relaxes from his closed-off body language and Link leans back against the wall a little closer to Carter instead of standing stiffly in the corner.

"Carter, about the way I left—"

The elevator stops again, and a group files in, large enough to crowd Link and him into opposite corners. Several conversations layered on top of each other fill the space. Carter catches fleeting glimpses of Link through the crowd. When the group exits at the lobby, Carter moves to follow, since he's parked on the street. But Link doesn't get out, so he doesn't. The doors close, and Carter turns to tell Link to not worry about what happened before, it's fine, old news.

Link speaks first, saying in a rush, "I shouldn't have left the way I did. It was an awful thing to do to you, and it was not your fault. It was me being a coward. I'm sorry. I totally understand if you want nothing to do with me." The elevator doors open on an underground garage lit by jumping fluorescent bulbs and sweeping headlights. Carter doesn't get a chance to respond. "This is my stop," Link says, sadness weighing their shoulders and voice. "It was really good to see you, Carter. Really. I hope you find what you're looking for here." When they step off, Carter follows, without deciding to. His legs move, his heart thumps, his stomach twists.

When he confronted Matthew at the condo, it had been two hurt people lashing out at each other. Matthew was defensive, laying the blame at Carter's feet and trying to center his own feelings by using Carter's forgiveness to make himself feel better. And Carter didn't want to give him the satisfaction. Carter, wounded, wanted to wound. It's the same way his family deals with conflict, the blueprint for every relationship he's ever had. That's not what Link is doing, though, their apology was honest, and so Carter can be honest too.

Starting over is fucking hard.

"I'm sorry as well," Carter calls out. A few feet away, Link stops. "I'm not great about being open with my feelings." To Link's unsurprised reaction he adds, "You may have noticed."

Link's full lips quirk at the corners. "Maybe a little." Even in the harsh, haunting lights of the parking garage, Link takes Carter's breath away. What Carter felt was real, but it was messy, and he needs to start from there.

"There was so much I wanted say, but I didn't know how," Link starts.

Carter nods. "I know. Me either. We were both in this really bizarre place; we were hurt and pretending and—I don't know about you, but I've never had to end a fake marriage before. I think we were bound to mess it up."

Link's smile stretches wider. "Fake divorce, I guess."

"Yes. Well, in that case," Carter says, "I'd like to request primary custody of the beignets."

Link's face twists into outrage. They set their hands saucily on their hips. "Uh. No way. You'll be hearing from my fake lawyer, mister." It's so nice, being able to joke around with Link again. It's nice to feel comfortable again, at least. Link gestures at a tiny, boxy red car at the end of the row. "Did you need a ride?"

He could use a ride, instead of leaving Paige to find a way home, but things feel too tentative right now, and it's best to leave on this first small step forward. "I should probably see what Paige wants to do," Carter says. "Unless she's staying the night." He involuntarily makes a face that Link chuckles at. Carter shakes his head, shooing that thought away. "I'll let her know I'm leaving and to call for a pickup. It's fine."

Link asks if he's sure, and Carter says that he is, and Link says they'd like to see him again sometime, and Carter says sure. And then it's awkward again when they both say goodbye and end up walking in the same direction because the street exit is next to Link's car. Link leans against the driver's side door and says, "Well."

Carter lifts to his toes and replies, "Well."

Link reaches out for a handshake. "See you around?"

"Mmhmm." Carter nods and takes Link's hand, so soft, those long fingers wrapped around Carter's palm that have been wrapped around other things on his body. Carter has a very ill-timed flashback. He's staring at Link's hand in his, staring in a way no one should be staring at a hand. He snaps his attention to Link's eyes, which are staring rather blatantly at Carter's lips. "I should… go…" Carter makes no motion to leave.

"Okay." Link says, eyes unfocused, licking across their lips.

They both move at the same time, meeting in the middle, crashing into each other, mouths meeting first in a hard kiss. Link's hands move up to cup Carter's face, and Carter lifts one hand to tangle in Link's long, thick hair and the other to curve around the dip of their waist. The kiss is messy and demanding and desperate. Carter captures Link's bottom lip between his own too eagerly, biting down instead of scraping his teeth lightly across as he'd meant to, and Link whimpers, surging suddenly against him, catching Carter off guard, and sending them both tripping backward. They bang against a car, tripping the alarm, then spring apart at the loud wailing.

Carter heaves a breath.

Link delicately wipes their slick, bitten-red mouth.

Carter clears his throat and smooths his shirt.

"Okay, well. 'Night," Link says.

"Yep. Yeah. Uh. Drive safe." Carter shoves his hands in his pockets and walks from the parking garage, slightly hunched over, lips tingling, heart pounding. That happened.

That was not supposed to happen.

TWENTY-THREE

PAIGE DOESN'T RETURN UNTIL EARLY the next morning. She pads upstairs and peeks into Carter's room. He's cross-legged, back propped against the wall, making one last run through a blueprint to ensure all the measurements are accurate and the codes all legal so construction can begin. After this, he'll have to tell his firm that he isn't coming back. And after that he'll have to find a new job.

"Good morning," he says.

The upstairs is flush with sunlight in the mornings, and Paige stops in a slanted beam of it. She's wearing the same thing she was last night, only much more disheveled.

"Morning."

She smiles. Carter hasn't stopped smiling since last night. "Sorry for ditching you. Were you able to get home okay?"

Paige squints, puzzled. "Obviously I did. Why do you look so happy, what's your angle?" She looks above and around her, panicked. "Are there more spiders? Are you keeping me here until one drops on my head? Is there one on my head, Carter?" She frantically smacks at her head and spins around.

"There's no—" Carter sighs and goes back to his work. "I'm just in a good mood. Or I *was*. Anyway, thank you for making me go out last night. I could have done without the water torture and threats, but you were right. And I'm glad I went."

Paige's head tilts, and she squints at him again. Her hair was already a mess when she came in. And after the spider panic, it's standing up in frizzy tufts. He wants to make fun of her, but he's trying to move past that.

"You're welcome or whatever," Paige finally says. "I'm gonna change."

As she thumps around in the bathroom, Carter congratulates himself on having an entirely pleasant interaction with his sister. Things *can* be different for him.

"By the way," Paige sticks her head out of the other bedroom to yell across the hall. "I heard about your makeout in the parking garage. Classy."

Carter says nothing, and takes out his phone to snap a picture of her hair in its disastrous state. He holds up the picture. "I'm posting this all over social media."

She scowls. "Like you even know how."

"Suit yourself," Carter says, and goes back to his work. After wrestling for his phone for a while, Carter agrees to delete the picture if she goes and gets breakfast. It's hardly even a win because Carter is paying for it, but she looks put out enough to satisfy him.

They eat biscuits and eggs with little cartons of orange juice in the camping chairs set up in the living room. It's been stripped to the original wood floors and plaster walls; both are desperately in need of refurbishing before he brings in any furniture. "Maybe I'll start with a table," Carter says. Greasy wax paper is spread across his knees to catch biscuit crumbs.

"Finally decided what to do with the place?" Paige sits cross-legged, not bothering to worry about getting crumbs everywhere as she eats with one hand and texts with the other.

"Not really." In his time here so far, what Carter keeps coming back to is how complex New Orleans is, how it exists at the intersection of so many things that shouldn't work, but somehow do. "Eclectic, I think." And suddenly he knows just the place to start.

Paige has been to Eli and Link's studio, so she inputs the address to his phone after he asks her to write it on a piece of paper and she rolls her eyes, asking him to "Please join us in the twenty-first century, Carter."

The studio is in a big warehouse next to a noisy train overpass and surrounded by a large gravel-filled lot. Metal sculptures line the front, and interesting graffiti covers the exterior walls. Carter didn't really know what to expect of a metalworking studio—a showroom? Link at a desk with a little soldering tool? He enters the wide-open bay door, and whatever expectations he may have had, Carter is not at all prepared for Link's long, nimble form in black coveralls and a black space-agey helmet with a full-face mask, perched on a stepladder, holding a blowtorch, and blasting fire at what looks like gaping fanged jaws.

It's the sexiest thing Carter has ever seen.

"Carter Jacob!" Link carefully puts the blowtorch down and pushes the mask up, revealing cheeks glowing red from the heat and dewy skin. Their hair is pulled back and damply matted. A bead of sweat trails down a tendon in their neck. *Oh god.* Link hops down from the ladder and jogs over, tugging off thick yellow gloves. "What are you doing here?"

"I…" Did he come here to be turned on by a sweaty Link wielding fire like a sexy wizard? No, that can't be right. "Oh. I came to commission something from you."

Link sends him a flirty look. "Oh?"

"Um." Carter forgets again why he came. "Oh. Yes! A table."

"Ah." Link pouts a bit at that, then lifts a shoulder, and removes the protective helmet entirely, setting it on a scorched wooden counter littered with small welding tools, twists of coil and wire, and seemingly random hardware. "Well then, let's make you a table."

Link leads the way to a back office, passing several works in progress, some with forms Carter can recognize, some that just look like twisted snarls of metal. The back half of the warehouse appears to be Eli's space, with an open kiln that is currently cold, various clamps and rugged metal shears and other unfamiliar tools, a spinning work wheel, and clear glass tubes in a variety of sizes and colors.

"No Eli today?" Carter says, curious but much more interested in the slinky stride of Link walking in front of him.

"He's out delivering to some stores that stock his pieces." Link sweeps out a hand in an *after you* gesture. Carter goes first into the cramped office.

"That's nice for him."

"It is," Link agrees, sitting at a desk made from metal pipes and a thick, trapezoidal sheet of aluminum that looks almost like an airplane wing. "Eli has worked really hard to be where he is. Now, what can I do to you—" Link blushes. "I mean. Do for you."

Carter looks at his hands, trying to hide a grin. The office is in a dark, dingy corner, yet the space is bright and inviting. "I don't have anything in mind. I trust your artistic vision." He looks up from beneath his eyelashes and confesses, "I mostly just wanted to see you," because now he knows Link is more than okay with him being here, and he's trying to be more honest. Carter can't resist the hope that he and Link can fall back into step.

"Just when I think you can't get any sweeter," Link closes the sketchbook they'd just opened. "Well, I have some ideas for your table, but right now, I have something else I'd like to do."

"Oh." Carter stands. Jeez, he just dropped into Link's workplace in the middle of the workday without warning, demanding Link see him and make something for him. "Sorry. I'll go. I didn't mean to interrupt." There's probably a waiting list for Link's work, as talented as they are.

"Carter." Link holds out a hand to Carter, laughing. "Come with me."

TWENTY-FOUR

TOGETHER THEY CLANG UP A metal staircase to a closed-off loft space above the office. Link opens a door, then tugs their hair loose and unzips the top half of their protective coveralls, tying the sleeves around their waist to reveal a thin, tight tank top underneath. "Oh, wow," Carter says, eyes wide and mouth parted. "Gosh, I love the use of the existing steel I-beams to create divisions in the space." The loft is an open L-shape, tucked in a corner of the warehouse; it was probably a space for machinery or control panels in the warehouse's original iteration.

Link's eyes light up. "I thought you might like it."

Carter continues to take in the space. The cement floors are gray, and the walls are white, but the beams and joists that are set in a basic grid throughout the loft have been painted in various bright shades: red around the dedicated living room space, blue around the kitchen, purple for an office with a desk built right into the beams, orange for a closed-in bathroom, yellow for an open bedroom space. "You live here?"

Link perches on the corner of a sofa with one leg crossed over the other and arms loose as they track Carter's exploration, asking with a coy head tilt, "Do you approve, Mister Architect?"

The furniture is all metalwork in clean lines and simple shapes, topped with cushions and fabrics in bold, colorful patterns. Like Eli's apartment, artwork is infused into the space without making it cluttered. And it manages to still be homey, which isn't easy to do in an industrial steel warehouse. "Well, the building is likely a prefab," Carter muses. "Built for durability, low overhead costs, and speed of construction. Certainly fits in with Sullivan's 'form follows function' principles."

Link lifts one eyebrow. "And that is…"

Carter strolls to a bookshelf built flush into a wall. Nestled among the books are colorful vases and bowls that Carter recognizes as Eli's work. "Basically, it means the essence of a building should be determined by its intended function or purpose. In other words, a warehouse looks like a warehouse, functions as a warehouse, *is* a warehouse." He sweeps an arm out to indicate the space. "A home should feel like a home, look like a home, function like a home."

"So," Link says. "That's a yes?"

"That's a yes." Carter moves back to the living room area, stopping just at Link's crossed legs, daring to lightly draw a finger around one knee, testing the waters. "Of course, even Sullivan considered the theory to be too dogmatic. After all, if we only designed for function, we'd all be out of a job pretty quickly." He himself has a secret flair for Art Nouveau ornamentation. Carter walks two fingers up Link's leg. "And you *know* my weakness for ornate French Creole and Italianate decorations."

Link's legs uncross, bracketing Carter's hips; ankles tucking around and pulling him closer. "*God*, enough dirty talk. Kiss me."

Carter kisses Link with slow drags of his lips and tongue. Warmth pools pleasantly in Carter's belly; his thumbs caress the line of Link's jaw. Link's palm slips beneath the back of Carter's shirt, and Carter moves in closer, breathing Link in, no longer shocked at how deeply and instantly Carter falls when his lips touch Link's, willingly giving himself over entirely—

Link pulls back, putting their foreheads together and pulling in a steadying breath. "In the interest of starting off on the right foot this time, I just—" They blink up at Carter, so close Carter can catalogue the flecks of green and yellow and brown in each iris. "I moved so quickly with Jamie, and it blew up in my face. I don't think I can go through that again, and I—"

"That's fine," Carter reassures. He strokes a thumb across Link's cheekbone. "We're just..." What did Eli say he and Paige were doing? "We're hanging out, right? It doesn't need to be anything more than that." Carter would almost believe himself if the words hadn't stuck in his throat like barbs. He wants this to be more, but he's not sure exactly what that would mean, so when Link asks, "Are you sure?" Carter nods and loses himself in Link's lips. Keeping things casual would be a lot easier if kissing Link didn't mean getting pulled headlong into an undertow.

Carter pulls away this time, intent on putting some space between their bodies, but he can't resist ducking in and dragging his lips across Link's throat to taste the lingering salty tang of sweat. Link moans into Carter's ear and scratches fingernails across his back.

He wants to drown in Link.

Moving away to catch his breath, Carter gathers Link's hair and tucks it behind one shoulder, exposing their neck and jaw and ear for Carter's mouth; he bends forward, then something catches his eye. The far back window pane has been replaced, and, instead of clear, flat glass it's done in colorful textured circles. Carter squints to figure out what the arrangement of colors is meant to be. "That's interesting."

Link, dazed, with slow blinks and glassy eyes, says, "*Interesting* is not the word I'd choose." Then they follow Carter's gaze to the back of the loft. "Oh, that."

Carter walks closer to see the details of the glass, the way the circles are arranged, then reaches out to touch the ridges and bumps and indentations. The floor below is dappled in little pools of blue and green. "They're wine bottles? The bottom part, right? Is it meant to be flowers or… a forest?"

"I don't think it's meant to be anything in particular," Link says, coming to stand next to him; their fingers brush Carter's hip.

Carter's never been one for abstract art. He feels uncultured and simple when he can only see the details and never the full picture as the artist intended. He needs art to look like something. He drops his hand from the glass, feeling silly. "Oh."

Link scans Carter's face for a long, searching moment. Looking back at the window, shoulders swaying a bit, Link comments blandly, "Jamie made that."

"Oh. She was an artist too?" That makes sense.

"She dabbled, I guess. Jamie spent a lot of time trying to figure out what she wanted and who she was. I don't know how much that had to do with your... with Matthew. I hope she figured it out." Link's tone sounds pained. Carter was naïve to think that Matthew and Jamie would stop coming up.

"Have you spoken to her?"

Link moves away from the window. "No. Clean break."

Carter slides his feet so a halo of green falls over his shoe. "I saw Matthew."

As they shrug back into the top half of the fireproof coveralls, Link, expression flat, flicks their eyes over Carter's face. Without meaning to, Carter put distance back between them. If he and Link are really going to start off on the right foot and do this correctly, they both probably have to start with the people who brought them here. "We should talk about this."

"I know," Link says. "How was it? Seeing him again?"

Carter moves his foot in and out of the little green circle. He could tell Link the full truth: that finally confronting Matthew helped him to realize that by trying so hard to be someone Matthew could love, he'd lost himself. He could also tell them that the week he spent with Link because of that was happier than the seven years he'd spent with Matthew. When he's with Link, he feels found. Confessing that is too much too soon.

Carter finally decides on, "It's complicated."

TWENTY-FIVE

CARTER TACKLES THE KITCHEN REMODEL first, because it's the smallest space with the least involved projects; other than the floor, he needs appliances and a fresh coat of paint on the cabinets after sanding them. The countertops are soapstone, which ages beautifully and just needs a bit of a polish. On the day his new oven arrives, Carter starts on a backsplash made of ceramic tiles in comforting neutral tones. He's just gotten the little square tiles all lined up on the counter when Eli and Paige come back from a date. Eli plunks a cooler filled with beer and ice on the counter and nods at the rows of tiles laid out face down and ready for mortar.

"What's this?" He moves a tile out of place; Carter frowns and puts it back.

"Backsplash."

"Do you even know what you're doing?" Paige asks, hauling herself up on the counter, taking out a beer, and bumping several tiles out of the way, probably on purpose. Carter's frown deepens. "In a sense," he replies, moving the tiles back. "How hard can it be?" He's not exactly an interior designer, but if he can plan out all the fiddly details of building a whole house, a kitchen backsplash should be no problem.

Eli accepts a beer from Paige, opens both of their bottles with an opener attached to his keychain, then points with the open top of his beer to the wall above the oven. "Well, how are you planning on arranging them? What sort of pattern?"

Carter looks at the wall, looks at the tiles, looks at the wall. "A... next to each other pattern?"

Eli gives a dismayed-sounding grunt, sips his beer, and looks at Paige, who says, "Now you see what I mean."

Eli nods and adds, "They're a little boring, too."

"That makes sense," Paige informs Eli, "because *Carter* is so boring."

Carter crouches to open his bucket of mortar. "I'm starting to understand what you two see in each other," he mumbles. Then, louder, "Doesn't Eli have his own home where you can go and not have to suffer through my boring and patternless backsplash?"

Link is coming by with the finished table soon, even more reason for them go away. But they ignore him. Paige swings her legs, and Eli leans on the counter next to her. She fixes his hair and calls him "E," and he toys with the seam of her sleeve, and they're really cute and really in his way. Carter gets the first line of tiles in place, then stands back to size it up. It looks fine. Clean and simple and classic and—"It's boring."

Eli and Paige "Mmhmm" in unison. Eli snaps his fingers. "I've got something in the car. Hold on." He's barely gone long enough for Carter to scowl in Paige's general direction before he returns with a small wooden crate and Link.

"Oh," Carter says. "I didn't hear you drive up."

"Had to park down the street." Link, out of breath and clutching one side, leans in the doorway. "Suddenly really wish you'd asked for bookends or something. Whew." Carter drops the trowel, heedless of the quick-dry mortar still smeared across it, and rushes to help drag the table the rest of the way in. It's round and not huge, but heavy and awkward, with spindly stems grasping the top like vines. No, like branches.

"It's a tree," Carter says. The base of the table has a wide, textured trunk, and the top is set on branches that are tipped with shining silver leaves. It reminds Carter of the tree they picnicked under the first day he and Link spent together—or, the first sober day they spent together. Carter still barely remembers the actual first day. He crouches to inspect the table; it's made of copper tubing, he thinks, and reshaped springs, and cuts of metal siding for the leaves. "Wow, a tree. Thanks," he says.

Link nods.

"That's Carter-speak for he loves it, and he loves you," Paige calls out.

Carter's neck goes hot, Link looks ready to bolt out the door, and Paige says, to a look from Eli, "What?"

"Uh. Hey," Eli says, shaking the crate he's still holding. "I have some leftover custom tiles. Carter, why don't you pick some out, and we'll spruce up that backsplash?"

A couple of hours and several beers later, Carter's house has a backsplash of simple, classic tiles with a little eclectic flair thrown in. They sit together around Carter's new table, Carter on the overturned mortar bucket and Link in one camping chair, Eli in the other with Paige draped sideways across his lap. The house is open to the mild evening: a soft breeze, chirping crickets, and the quiet noise of the neighbors going about their lives.

He and Link and Eli are talking about a boutique that wants to feature some of Link's work for "exposure" and no pay, when Paige, who had been unusually quiet, blurts, "So what's the deal here?" She gestures between Carter and Link. "'Cause we're all bored with the 'will they, won't they' thing."

Link, perhaps still unused to Paige, stares at her, eyes wide. Carter sighs and replies mildly, "Paige, have you ever considered minding your own business?"

She crosses her legs over Eli's knees. "Not really."

Eli tries to change the subject to some issue he's having with the owner of the warehouse, but Paige looks too unrepentant and Carter is too panicked about the look on Link's face. Carter is already walking a very tentative line lest Link get spooked and run off again; he is trying so hard to not be pushy, and here Paige just—

"Who is 'we,' anyway?" Carter says, when Eli's story pauses.

Paige kicks a foot in the air. "Like, the royal we. You know."

Carter leans forward in his chair to tell Paige exactly where she can stick her *royal we*, when Link finally speaks up. "We're just… hanging out." Their tone is off. Carter tries to read why in Link's expression. Is that not what Link wants? Is Carter still being too pushy? He should never have dropped by and asked Link to make the table for him. Carter's stomach twists anxiously, and he turns his turmoil onto Paige.

"Since when do you care about my love life? Other than disapproving of it."

"You're my brother, Carter." She pivots, legs dropping to the floor. "Of course I care."

Carter's arms cross; he leans away as she leans closer. "You certainly have a funny way of showing it." He's being defensive and unfair, aiming to wound. Paige has been really supportive lately, and he'd rather leave all of their antagonistic-sibling history behind; yet it stubbornly stays, weighing down the present. Perhaps there is no such thing as starting over.

Link's fingers drum on the table, breaking the silence. "So, the landlord?"

"Oh. Yeah," Eli says. "So the dude calls and—"

"You were just so... *you*," Paige interrupts, as if there hadn't been an obvious attempt to move the conversation to less uncomfortable subjects. "And I couldn't understand why you wouldn't just, like... stop. Why you made things so hard for yourself." She hops off Eli's lap, then drags the cooler from the kitchen to the table, puts it next to Carter, and sits on it sideways. "I thought, like, maybe if I was hard enough on you, you'd try to fit in. Stop getting picked on at school and at home. I spent so much time making excuses for you, you have no idea."

It's an old hurt; stale and scabbed over, but not gone. "Sorry that who I am as a person was so difficult for you, Paige."

"That's not—*urg*." She looks at Eli, who grimaces and shrugs. She blows out a loud, frustrated breath. "That's not what I'm saying. I am saying..."

Carter waits, arms still crossed defensively, for her to continue about what a burden he apparently was in front of Link and Eli, who are both are very clearly wishing they were anywhere else.

"I am saying that I was wrong."

Carter sits up with a start. "What?" She was *what*?

"Don't make me say it again." She rolls her eyes, without actual contempt, perhaps even at herself. "Honestly, I… I admire that you don't care what other people think about you, who you are, who you date, what you're interested in, what you wear. I worry about you and I haven't always handled that worry appropriately, and I…" She sighs heavily. "…am sorry."

She is *what*?

"Oh. I. Okay." Carter looks from Paige to Eli, who is smiling at her with a mix of pride and fondness and an intimacy that makes Carter quickly look away, to Link, who is looking at Carter with a soft, encouraging smile. His heart trips in his chest.

"I guess I… I haven't always been very kind to you, either. So, I am also sorry." There's a moment of new understanding. It's nice, but Carter doesn't want to hug her or anything. The past is still the past, so he nods, for a start. Paige nods.

Eli says, "Aw, what a sweet sibling moment."

Paige makes a gagging noise, and Carter *hmphs*.

"Welp, I need to get home and get some sleep," Eli says, coming over to tug Paige up from the cooler and winding an arm around her shoulders. They go upstairs to say goodbye. Carter is finally alone with Link, as he'd hoped to be all evening.

"I should probably get going, too," Link says.

"Oh." Carter nods, too much and too fast. "Yeah, of course. It's late." He heaves himself up from the bucket to walk Link to the door. It feels like the other moment just before they'd ended up all over each other, that pull toward Link, that connection tugging them closer and closer. Carter holds back, and Link shifts awkwardly, then pecks Carter on the cheek, jogs down the front steps and calls, "Talk to you soon."

As he's trying and failing to fall asleep, Carter contemplates exactly how slow is slow, because it's starting to feel as if he and Link are going in reverse. He blames Paige and her big mouth. He rolls over on his side. No, that's not fair; he blames himself. Next to his sleeping bag,

Carter's phone lights up with a message. Hoping it's Link wanting to continue the evening after all, Carter grabs for it. But it isn't a message from Link. It's a picture from Matthew.

TWENTY-SIX

THE PLEASANTLY WARM SPRING WEATHER is turning less pleasant by the hour, and Carter is adjusting to the deep South's heat and humidity in the same way a lobster adjusts to being boiled alive.

The house still has a long way to go, and Carter's progress slows as he fights through the stifling weather in a home without air-conditioning. On the warmest morning yet, he gives up on hauling out old carpet and wall paneling—too hot for any of that—and sets up his laptop on the kitchen counter next to the largest window and the strongest fan in the house. Paige comes downstairs in a long sleeve shirt with the sleeves rolled up, jeans rolled up to her knees, and hair in a ponytail beneath one of Eli's baseball hats.

"Off for a morning of clam-digging?" Carter comments.

"I did not pack a summer wardrobe; it gets hot too soon here."

"Feel free to leave," Carter replies, reflexively grouchy. They're supposed to be better than this now. "Sorry, no. It is hot." Still, how long does she plan on crashing with him? Doesn't she have friends and a life to get back to? At some point soon this thing with Eli will have run its course, as her relationships always do.

Paige complains about the heat again, then about Carter having no air-conditioning as well as no refrigerator, and then leans against the counter next to him. "Whatcha up to?"

He angles the screen of his laptop. "Applying for a job," he says, then clarifies, "A *job* is a place where money comes from. You should try it." His boss at his old firm put him in touch with a similar firm in New Orleans. He hopes they have an opening, as he really needs the cash flow if he's ever going to get this house into shape.

Paige kicks the back of Carter's knee so his leg buckles. "So hilarious," she says, deadpan, then waves a hand to indicate the house. "I thought you were doing this for a job."

Carter frowns. "No, this is just for fun, I guess."

"Hmm," Paige says. "If you say so. And actually, I have plans. Big plans."

Carter makes a vague noise of quasi-interest and hunches over to finish polishing his résumé and cover letter. A minute ago, this job seemed like a great idea. It pays well; he already knows how to do it; it has a pretty solid dental plan. His fingers hover over the keyboard. Suddenly, full coverage for crowns and root canals doesn't seem quite as appealing.

"Carter! Don't you want to know my plans?" Paige pinches his elbow.

"Ow. Okay."

"Yay!" She claps her hands, pushes up from the counter, and then holds her palms up flat next to her face as if framing it. "Picture it: Paige T. Jacob, Artist Agent." She moves her hands, framing her face from different angles with eyes and smile wide as she poses.

"Huh," Carter says.

Paige's hands drop. "That's it? 'Huh.' Come on, Carter. Be happy for me."

Carter huffs in exasperation and closes his laptop. He's clearly not going to finish this job application today, now that the morning has become all about Paige. "I don't know," Carter says. "What do you even know about art? You represented pharmaceuticals. It's not exactly the same thing." He's not trying to be harsh, but a better use of her skills would be to find another drug company that's hiring. There have been too many flights of fancy around here lately.

"Okay, first of all." Paige holds up one finger. "I can sell anything to anyone because I'm that good. Two." A second finger snaps up to join the first. "I have excellent taste and I *know* retail. And tres, I've been spending a lot of time with Eli and Link and their artist friends, and they're all so talented but, like, they have no idea how to sell themselves.

Eli is lucky and he hustles, working himself to the ground to get the reputation around town that he has, but it shouldn't be like that." She shrugs; a little of her righteous anger fizzles out. "I think I could really help and I think I'd be really good at it. And I want to do it here. In New Orleans."

"Okay," Carter says, trying to be supportive. She will probably be good at it, now that he thinks about it, but, "How can you afford to start a business?"

"I took out a loan." She toys with her hair and avoids eye contact.

"You took out a loan," Carter repeats. "With your credit?"

"Okay, fine. Dad gave me a loan."

"Wow." Carter is genuinely impressed. Their father is absurdly tightfisted; Paige really can sell anything.

"And don't worry, I'll find my own place." Paige says, patting his shoulder. "I don't want to camp out in your sad house any more than you want me here. Eli thinks I'll like the part of town where he lives. Little more modern, you know. We're pretty excited about all of this."

Carter smiles. He's actually proud of Paige these days. She's still herself, irritatingly so, but she's grown. "So you and Eli are a 'we,' huh? Or are we still talking about the royal we?"

"Shut up," Paige says with a laugh. She shoves him so hard he crashes into the counter. Somewhere around age thirteen, Carter grew taller than her, but it's never hampered her ability to kick his ass. "And what about you and Link?" she demands. "Are you a we? You never answered me."

Carter rights himself, rubbing at his waist where it collided with the counter's edge. "I don't know what we're doing," he answers honestly. "We've done everything out of order, and it's confusing. And to make it more complicated, look what Matthew sent me last night."

He pulls his phone from his pocket and opens his messages to a picture of the two of them, him and Matthew, posing on a beach at St. Barts, happy and tan and arm in arm. Paige peers closely at the picture, then recoils in horror.

"Carter, that bathing suit is so small! My eyes!"

Carter snatches his phone back. "Forget about the bathing suit."

"I wish I could," Paige says, pained.

"Just." Carter sighs. "Why do you think he sent me a picture of us? It means he was thinking about me, right? So, what? He wants to get back together?" Carter doesn't want that. But then, he didn't delete the picture right away, either.

"Who cares." Paige says, taking the phone and deleting the picture for him. "You forget about Matthew, and I'll forget the horror of seeing you in a bikini bottom." She shudders. "Now, I have some artists to agent."

She heads out of the door as Carter calls, "It was not a bikini bottom, it was a European swim trunk!" He looked *fine*. Still, he's glad she deleted it. Carter didn't even want to go to St. Barts, to some all-inclusive resort for couples only. He had fun; he isn't immune to tropical decadence and free-flowing drinks; but the entire thing felt false, decadence for the sake of decadence and forced romance around every corner. Of course, he knows now why it felt so fake.

Why didn't he delete the picture?

An electric sander sits in the corner, waiting for Carter to smooth years of nicks and scratches and worn footpaths from the floors. He goes for a walk instead. The sky is cloudless, the sun relentless. By the time Carter makes it through the neighborhood, past the trolley line, and into the small park where he likes to work sometimes, his shirt is soaked with sweat. This must be why Link's summer wardrobe favors tank tops and shirts that slink off their shoulders and are cut off at their ribs. Carter sits on a bench by the lake and fans his shirt away from his damp, sticky torso. Thinking about Link's wardrobe and its lack of coverage isn't helping cool him off.

The art museum sits, elegant and gleaming white, on a hill next to the park. Carter goes in today for the first time, into the blessedly cool grand hallway. The interior and exterior are done entirely in a Neoclassical style, in the Beaux-Arts tradition seen in countless government buildings and museums across the country. Carter has always found the style beautiful—with all its symmetrical arches and columns, dramatically vaulted ceilings, grandiose balconies, sweeping stairways, and polished white marble—if a bit cold and rigid, and needlessly showy.

He wishes Link were here so he could tell them about the connection between Beaux-Arts architecture and American colonialism, and Link could explain what he's supposed to be seeing, or not seeing, in the artwork. Carter strolls past the Renaissance art, the historical wing, then moves through more modern collections. His footsteps are silent on the carpet, and he feels out of place and out of time as he takes in pieces he seems to understand less and less.

Carter stops at a painting with blobs and splatters of color, tilts his head, squints one eye. He holds his hands up in a frame as Paige did to her own face, then drops them when it doesn't help to clarify anything. Carter wants it to *be* something, the painting. He likes when things make sense. *It isn't supposed to be anything in particular,* Link said, and perhaps that's Carter's entire problem. He's trying to make sense of everything instead of letting it be.

•

TWENTY-SEVEN

THE HOT, HUMID WEATHER CONTINUES to get hotter and more humid, and the progress on Carter's house continues to be painstakingly slow. He gets a job offer from the local firm he applied to, and Paige nets enough clients to move out. Her stuff arrives from Aurora on a moving truck in the afternoon of a day that hits ninety-nine degrees. Carter and Eli and Eli's very tall and very muscular friend Malcolm haul furniture and boxes up four flights of stairs.

"Just put that in the corner," Paige says from the galley kitchen, arranging dishes in the white cabinets she insisted were a must-have. Carter puts a heavy side table in the corner; his back aches and his arms are weak from so much strain.

"The other corner," Paige calls. Carter grits his teeth and moves it to the other back corner. "No. Carter. The *other* corner, by the couch. Come on, use that brain of yours."

Eli puts a box on the dining room table and gives Paige one of those couple-looks that communicates something they've clearly discussed at length.

Paige dramatically rolls her eyes. "I mean, that corner is fine. I'll move it later. Thank you for helping, Carter. You can go if you want." She looks at Eli, who nods happily, then adds, "I know you were super busy buffing that one spot on your living room floor that you've been buffing for two weeks."

"Sanding," Carter replies, pushing the table tightly into the wrong corner, then setting a heavy box of books on top. He'd like to see her move *that*. "I'm not buffing it; I'm sanding it. Buffing merely removes the top layer of polyurethane sealant for surface damage issues. *Sanding* is for deeper wood damage; it is more extensive and takes longer."

Paige gestures with a frustrated chop of her hand from Carter to Eli. "See?" she says. Eli shakes his head in dismay, but Carter isn't sure which one of them it's directed at.

Malcolm brings up the last boxes, and he and Eli and Carter sit on still-askew furniture with bottles of water as Paige buzzes around, rearranging and unpacking. "Place is nice," Malcolm says. He's an artist, too. Watercolor, he said.

The place is a standard-looking apartment, not unlike Paige's standard-looking apartment back in Aurora. It's nicer, though: newer, bigger, with updated appliances and a garden tub, and a saltwater pool in the courtyard. Somehow, Paige followed him to a place she'd never been with no plans and no prospects and accidentally became a better version of herself. Meanwhile, Carter has been buffing the same ten-square-foot patch of floor for weeks. *Sanding.*

"What's Link up to today?" Carter asks, aiming for casual as he presses the cool bottle to his neck. He and Link have seen each other socially, at gatherings to watch sports, group get-togethers at bars, and that one chain burger restaurant where everyone seems to end up. Carter stays on the periphery, and Link stays busy, talking to everyone, everyone except for Carter as Link has been keeping a careful distance. Carter could almost measure the exponentially greater space between them every time he and Link cross paths.

"Still working on that big piece," Eli says with a shrug.

Malcolm is sitting on Paige's yellow sunflower settee. It's fascinating to think of someone that hulking working on an art form as delicate as watercolor painting. "Wait, I thought that was done," Malcolm says. "The snake thing, right?"

Eli turns with an eyebrow raised. "Not quite," he says, terse.

Malcolm's dark eyes cut over to Carter. "Ohh… right, right. My bad."

Carter removes the water bottle from his neck and stares at the water inside. So he wasn't imagining it. Link really doesn't want to see him. But hasn't he been respectful of Link's boundaries? Hasn't he taken things slow, the way Link wanted? He's made peace with their relationship being suspended in ambiguity. Hasn't he?

Paige comes bustling in. "I need two of you to help me move the bed. I changed my mind; I want the headboard in front of the windows."

Carter stands. "I really should go back to sanding, so." He drops the water bottle in the recycling bin that's now tucked neatly away in the kitchen, and moves the box of books off the table, then moves the table next to the couch. In one afternoon, Paige's new home will be mostly settled. Carter hasn't felt at home in nearly half a year.

"Hey, Carter, wait."

Carter grimaces at the threshold of the open door. He's tired and hot and completely out of patience for her bossiness. "*What.*"

"Okay, wow." Paige holds her hands up in defense. "Surly today." She gives him a card that's painted blue and decorated with hand-drawn sketches of yellow fireworks surrounding a red sun. On the back in block letters is the *who what where when* of a party invitation. "We're having a housewarming slash celebrating my new career slash summer solstice party at the warehouse. You should come."

"I'll think about it," he says, intentionally noncommittal. He doesn't want to be here; he doesn't want to go to a party; he just wants to be miserable alone. He starts to leave again. Paige stops him by slamming the door in front of his face. Carter sighs. "Paige, I need a shower and some ibuprofen. I can't think about a party right now."

Paige's face softens. "Please, Carter?" She even touches his arm. "None of this would have happened without you. I want you there to celebrate too. And some of my friends are coming from Aurora. Meredith will be there. She still likes you for some reason. Come on."

Carter almost agrees just so he can leave, and Paige will stop being so unsettlingly nice to him. *Almost.* "I dunno..."

"There will be so much alcohol, I promise."

"Okay," Carter says, finally making his escape and stepping into the breezeway. "But I'll be in a bad mood the whole time. and you can't stop me."

Paige says, "I wouldn't expect anything less," before the door clicks closed with a settled finality.

Then all Carter has left is his house. And all his house has is its good bones: the solid, sturdy construction that still waits to be something new. He sits in the dark on his sleeping bag, sweaty and irritable, well into the evening. He's alone. It's not a relief, yet it's not as terrifying as he'd feared. It's just, well, lonely. Is this what Eli was talking about? Does it get worse or better from here? He wants to talk to Link about nothing and everything, wants to know what he did wrong. But when he thumbs open his contacts, he pulls up Matthew's name and scrolls to the message he never answered about the picture Paige deleted.

That was fun, Carter replies to the text about their luxury beach resort vacation. It's not even true, really. At least Matthew is trying. A reply comes immediately.

How are you?

He's never been so lost in his entire life.

I'm fine, he texts back. It's also a lie, but a familiar one. In that way, it's comforting.

I wish I could see you in person, Matthew sends back.

Carter's fingers hover over the keyboard. He frowns at the glowing screen. It would be easy enough. It would be close enough to happiness that Carter could stop feeling so alone and adrift and unwanted. He doesn't need Paige here to tell him that Matthew only wants him because he's lonely too.

At least they were lonely together.

Carter shuts off the phone and tries to sleep in the sweltering upstairs of his perpetually unfinished house.

TWENTY-EIGHT

As Carter approaches the warehouse for Paige's party, fire blasts in sprays from behind the roof. It's not the controlled, steady burn of Link's soldering tool, but wide, wild arcs flaring across the dark sky. Carter parks across the street beneath the train overpass. The gravel lot around the warehouse is packed with cars, and even from here the rapid beat of drums carries loud and clear, with whoops and laughter joining the sound as he walks closer. Carter balances a flat plastic container in both arms and follows the noise and flashes of light around to the back.

It's nearly as raucous as the street party Link took Carter to on his last night in New Orleans, way back in February before they—before he—before. There's a drum circle and people in costume walking on stilts above the crowd, a cleared area with fire spinners and fire hula-hooping and fire breathers, and a stage where performers are spinning and dancing on silks suspended from rafters. Carter's pace slows, then stops. It's both too dark and too bright, too busy, so much going on that he can't process it all.

Even on this hot night after a hot day, he endured a hot oven and made cupcakes for the party. He anticipated a gathering of Link and Eli's usual group of friends that Carter still feels weird around, that they'd all hang out and watch sports and eat snacks, but this? This is a *party*. Carter blinks down at his container of cupcakes, feeling suddenly very small and very silly. He takes a step back. He wishes he hadn't made cupcakes. He wishes he hadn't come. He spots Link, who is rolling a non-flaming hula hoop around one arm as they talk to a few people. Carter goes unnoticed. He takes another step back. Paige crosses in front of Link, hand in hand with Eli, stops to chat, then moves on to talk to someone else. Some of her friends from Aurora are mingling among the artsy crowd in a somehow seamless blend of Paige's two worlds.

It's always been this way with them: Paige fits in, she adapts. Paige swans through life with an ease that has always escaped Carter. That same ease was one of the most appealing things about Matthew, initially. That Carter could attach himself to someone so naturally likable, so he could be too. On his own, Carter isn't interesting enough, not even with cupcakes. He isn't charming and popular like Matthew and Paige, he isn't creative and artistic like Link and Eli and their friends. He doesn't belong here. He doesn't belong anywhere. Carter turns to leave.

"Carter! Hi!" It's Meredith, Paige's friend who still likes him for some reason.

"Oh, hi." Carter shifts his cupcake container to one arm when Meredith gives him a side hug. "Good to see you."

"You aren't leaving, are you?" Meredith says, moving close to be heard over the noise. She's wearing a ruffled bohemian skirt; it has tiny bells that jingle with every slight movement. The invitation for the party said to dress "boho festive." Carter bought a polo shirt printed with pineapples, which was clearly off the mark, as he so often is.

Carter looks around for an excuse to leave. "I have a headache," he says. It sounds like a question. Meredith, of course, has aspirin in her purse. Carter swallows them dry; one lodges painfully in his throat. "Thanks," he croaks.

"Isn't this just a blast?" Meredith says. "Paige is *so* wild. I love her."

Carter lifts his head in a sort-of nod. He has no response for that. "I, um. I'm gonna set these down somewhere. Be right back?" He juggles the container to touch her shoulder in a way that's meant to be friendly and polite. She flutters her eyelashes and grabs his wrist.

"Uh," Carter says.

"Don't be a stranger tonight," Meredith says, releasing him with a wink and a smile.

Carter stumbles, walking into the churning belly of the festivities and then to the sidelines after he almost walks right into a fire spinner. There's an open bar, as Paige promised, but no food table. Carter has completely misjudged the parameters of this party. He finds a back door and ducks inside the warehouse to locate a garbage can and chuck his embarrassing cupcakes. It's nearly pitch-black inside, still noisy, but muted. Carter hasn't been to the warehouse enough to have memorized where the trash cans are, but he's hoping there's one in that back office. Leaning a hand on the wall to guide him, he makes his way.

He bumps into stairs. At the top, the door to Link's loft is open; the doorway is lit with soft yellow. Link certainly will have a trash can. Carter will just pop in and pop out, and it's not invasive and creepy because the door is open. He climbs the stairs and steps into Link's home, feeling creepy and invasive.

Swallowing hard, Carter quickly crosses the loft to the kitchen. The aspirin in his dry throat scratches like a thorn. Quickly getting a glass of water is probably okay. Carter places the cupcakes on the kitchen table, drinks a glass of water, and closes his eyes with relief.

"Hello?"

Carter jumps and yelps, dropping the glass. Fortunately, he was still standing over the sink, so it clatters loudly against the metal but doesn't break. Less fortunately, Link is standing in the kitchen now. Carter rushes to explain why he's in Link's kitchen, in Link's house, in the dark all by himself. Link doesn't want him here, that has been made very clear. What he says is, "I, uh, brought cupcakes. Sorry."

Link's eyes narrow and they flip on the kitchen lights. Carter blinks against the brightness, and, once his vision adjusts, he can see that Link is wearing glittery blue eyeliner to match glittery blue nails, short cutoffs, and one of those tight half-shirts. Carter stares down at the floor with heat creeping up his neck. He's embarrassed and ashamed and turned on.

"Sorry," he says again.

"Carter," Link says, sighing. "Why are you apologizing for cupcakes?"

Instead of replying that he doesn't know, or that he's really apologizing for crossing boundaries because he's uncomfortable and out of place at this party, and in this city, and also in Link's life, Carter stares at the floor and blurts out, "Do you not like me anymore?"

Link sighs again, and, from the corner of his eyes, Carter can see them twist their hair up in a bun, then let it fall loosely. "No, Carter. The opposite, actually."

Carter looks up as far as Link's leanly muscled legs. *So much leg.* "What does that mean?"

"It's embarrassing," Link says.

It can't possibly be more embarrassing than the pulse of heat in Carter's groin when he takes in the shift of Link's thighs. "Okay," Carter says, not wanting to push and struggling to form coherent thoughts. He looks up to the exposed skin of Link's stomach, then quickly away.

"Okay. No." Link's feet shuffle across the floor, closer. "Honestly? It's because I can't trust myself around you. I'm trying to take things slow, but it's so difficult, and you have no idea how much I want to kiss you, and more, right now."

Carter's eyes drag up, up, to Link's elegant neck and those wide, full lips. "I probably do," Carter says, voice strained. Link is beautiful and sexy and cool and interesting, and Carter can't imagine what about his own boring self could possibly be so appealing.

"Is there anything I can do? To be less… um, kissable," Carter asks.

"I doubt it," Link says with a long sigh. "I mean, you just called yourself kissable for one. And you brought cupcakes that you probably made yourself. And, oh, I just realized your shirt has little pineapples on it."

Carter plucks at the fabric. "It's festive."

Link's eyes close. "You're killing me."

Carter can't help it, he smiles. Outside the party rages on, but here with Link he's finally enjoying himself a little. He shouldn't need someone else to anchor him, he knows; he should find his own port in his own sea. But it's different than how it always was with Matthew, when he needed Matt to feel worthy. No, he needed Matthew to decide if he *was* worthy. When he's with Link, Carter feels as if he matters all on his own, just as he is.

"Do you want one? They're fresh citrus cupcakes with orange buttercream."

Link groans obscenely. "Fuck yes, I want one."

TWENTY-NINE

THEY BOTH EAT ONE CUPCAKE, then Link reaches for another. Carter scrapes little bits of orange buttercream frosting off the paper wrapper and licks it from his fingers. He's relieved that Link doesn't hate him and want him to go away, and maybe a tiny bit pleased at the reason for Link's distance.

"So, what are you doing up here?" Carter asks. "I mean, I know this is your home, but don't you want to get back to the party?"

Link is taking their time with the second cupcake. "Eh. I swear these gatherings get more elaborate every time. I love a good soirée, don't get me wrong, but I heard someone talking about getting a live elephant for their next party, I mean *really*. I just needed a break."

The noise of drums and jubilant partygoers, and the colors of stage lights and swirls of fire seep in from the darkened windows. In the right state of mind, Carter enjoys a good soirée himself. He'd much rather be with Link in this quiet space. "Do you want to watch TV or something?" Carter asks, trying to create the boundaries that he badly needs, as he stares at Link's throat swallowing the last bites of cupcake, and Link stares at Carter's frosting-tipped fingers moving in and out of his mouth.

"Yeah, sure. Well." Link's head swivels toward the center of the loft, where the bed waits, ready. "The television is in the bedroom. That might be, uh—"

"Right," Carter says. Climbing into bed together hasn't exactly kept things platonic in the past. "Do you have cards? We could play cards."

Link hunts down a pack of playing cards, and they both sit cross-legged on the couch, facing each other. "What are you in the mood for?" Links asks, shuffling the cards. "I mean, game-wise."

Carter adjusts more comfortably against an arm rest. "Whatever you want."

Link's eyebrows raise and fall, briefly. "Okay." They deal the cards and explain the rules for crazy eights, which Carter has heard of but never played. Link nods for him to go first. Carter plays a king of hearts. After two rounds that Link wins, Carter challenges them to a double-or-nothing final round. Outside, there's a pop and then the sky suddenly bursts with colorful lights. Carter *oohs* and Link tuts, "Of course there's fireworks."

The last time he and Link played cards there was rain outside the hotel room, rather than showers of sparks outside Link's loft, but the way Carter felt, as if he and Link existed together in some sort of bubble, some deeper connection he couldn't understand, he still feels that way. He's still trying to understand it.

"Link?" Carter says. Link hums, flicking down the three of spades. Carter nudges it neatly into place on the stack. "How would you explain art?"

Link's eyes narrow. "As in, explain all of art? How long do you expect this game to last, Carter Jacob?"

"No, I guess..." Carter plays the three of diamonds. "You make art that serves a purpose. It makes sense. But what about art that doesn't?"

Link's eyes carefully scan Carter's face; in the low light they look darker, the soft brown of cedarwood. "You mean that sincerely, don't you?" Carter isn't sure how to take that question, but Link's gaze is soft, their mouth upturned in a sweet smile. "All right, well. Isn't architecture a form of art? You find art in wrought iron gabling or those balustrade railings, right?"

It tugs in Carter's chest; the fact that Link not only actually did care about Carter's ramblings but remembered them. "Yes," Carter concedes. "But architecture necessitates function. Ornamentation is secondary and requires an underlying syntactical relationship to the building's primary function."

Link inhales sharply, eyes fluttering. "So then, I guess art sometimes is the opposite. The art itself conveys meaning. Or, the art *is* the meaning."

Carter plays a card. Art is the purpose or the purpose is art. It exists for itself and, because of that, has an inherent meaning. It's a compelling thought. "I suppose if one were to differentiate between ornamentation and decora—" Link's mouth crashes against Carter's, interrupting his upcoming monologue. Link scrambles closer. Cards scatter across the couch and the floor; Carter's last few fall from his hand. He cups Link's face, kisses back, and moves his legs so Link can settle in his lap. He pulls away just to ask, even though he really, really doesn't want to.

"Are you sure you want this?"

Link hovers over him, hair falling like a curtain, thumbs stroking down Carter's neck, eyes so dark and intense Carter has to look down and watch Link's mouth. "So sure," Link says, straddling Carter's lap and ducking back in for another kiss, then stopping to ask, "Wait, do you want to?"

Carter pretends to contemplate the question. "No, I'd rather talk about balustrades. Of course I want to."

Link takes another sharp breath and murmurs against Carter's lips, "God, say balustrades again." Carter does. Link moans and writhes against him.

There's so much warm, smooth skin available to Carter's roving hands already, with Link's cutoff shorts and T-shirt. His fingers travel up Link's spine, the curve of their back, up the length of Link's strong thighs and slide beneath the jagged cut of their shorts, first the top, then around to the back to skim the curve of their ass. Link gasps, hips shifting. Carter's index finger slips in farther, finding hot, yielding skin.

"Yes," Link says, voice airy and trembling, head tilting back. "I want that, *yes*."

Carter can't do much with his hand twisted to reach inside the leg of Link's shorts, just lets Link kiss him and move against him as Carter's body yearns for more. Link grinds forward against Carter's groin, then back against his fingers, mouth falling open. "What do you want?" Link's head tilts to the side so Carter can mouth along the line of it. Carter's distracted reply, "Whatever you want," is apparently insufficient.

Link stands. Carter blinks and babbles. "What—why—what—"

"I can't deal with you sometimes," Link says, but it's with a fond smile. "Carter, sweetie. Consider this a… what was it? Syntactic relationship."

"Syntactical," Carter corrects. "It means—"

Link flutters a hand at him. "I love your explanations, but there's a time and place. If I'm not comfortable with something, I'll say so. And you should too. Now, what do you want?"

Carter takes a few breaths to clear his head, wipes damp palms on his legs, and has to look down at his lap when he replies, "I want to be inside of you."

THIRTY

CARTER HAS CERTAINLY BULLDOZED RIGHT through any and all boundaries with that confession and is even more convinced of this when Link holds up one finger and disappears into the bathroom. Alone on the couch, lust haze clearing, Carter becomes aware again of the party still carrying on, loud and bright, outside. Has anyone noticed he's gone? Paige, probably not. Meredith, likely. He feels momentarily bad for Meredith; she's had a bad run.

Link is taking a while. Should he leave?

"Take your pants off!" Link calls out from the bathroom. Carter complies and sits back on the couch in his underwear. He can't go very far without pants, so he's probably safe staying put. Link finally emerges from the bathroom in only snug, silky, black underwear hemmed in a thin strip of lace. It's definitely a different pair and Carter is definitely not going anywhere.

Link slinks into the room, switches the light off, then resumes their earlier position straddling Carter's lap. There's even more skin for Carter to touch. His kisses are harder, the urgency higher. Carter reaches blindly to Link's stomach, up to pinch the hardened nubs of their nipples. Link whines, hips bucking against Carter's, and moves back across Carter's knees, tugs Carter's underwear down, and rolls a condom onto him. Link's underwear comes off, too, flung away carelessly, somewhere behind the couch. "Still good?"

"Yes," Carter says, as Link shuffles forward again, lifted so Carter can kick his briefs off the rest of the way. "Are you?"

Still lifted, Link takes Carter's hand, guiding his fingers back to where Carter had been teasing at pushing inside before, now slick and yielding. "I am very ready," Link says, voice husky, body moving against Carter's, lining up; ready.

Carter holds himself steady as Link sinks slowly. His throat goes dry at the intense, tight heat. He wants to be less passive as Link wants, but he lets Link take charge, can't help it, closes his eyes and gives himself over completely.

Link lifts and falls, slowly at first, pecking Carter's lips and grasping his shoulders. Then the pace picks up, and Link's hands move to twist in Carter's hair, their legs spreading wider so Carter is buried deep inside. Link groans, lifts up, and Carter's hips buck helplessly, slamming into Link as they come back down.

"*Carter,*" Link moans. "*Carter, Carter.*"

Outside, presumably, the party is still going. For Carter, nothing exists right now outside of Link. He no longer cares to understand it or quantify it or figure it out. He's tried pretending they were something else, he's tried a clean break, he's tried keeping a friendly distance. Nothing makes sense except the way Carter feels when he's with Link.

Link shifts forward, rubbing against Carter's stomach, torso twisting as they lift and fall at a fast, uncoordinated pace. Carter thrusts up hard, and Link arches, head thrown back, lost to pleasure. Carter pumps inside one last time and comes. He presses his face into Link's neck, breathing raggedly as he cools down, lips and tongue working absently. Link goes still, then shakes and sighs and trembles.

"We're art, not architecture," Carter says, with Link draped limply beside him.

"Hmm?" Link replies, slow and sluggish.

Carter smiles. He doesn't need Link to understand; he said it for himself. It's enough, to know that Link desires him, that things are as they have always been between them, even if he's unable to say exactly what that is. It doesn't matter. Carter has spent too much of his life worrying about the practical functions of things instead of the irrational beauty of them. They both clean up and dress.

"I got a job offer," Carter says, stepping into his pants.

"That's great." Link is still hunting down their underwear behind the couch.

"Check the office area," Carter says, helpfully. "I don't know if I'm going to take it, though. The job, I mean. Not your underwear." Carter watches Link's naked backside walk into the bedroom. They seem to give up on the search and open a dresser drawer for new ones.

"Why not?" Link calls.

Carter pulls his pineapple shirt over his head. "Well, Paige thinks that I should do something different, like she is. In the name of not coming all this way to make the same mistakes, or something." It's easy for her to say, though, she's personable and plucky; he's weird and difficult. He also doesn't know what else he'd do.

Link comes back, fully dressed in comfy-looking pajamas. "Well, Paige is, let's say, *free with her opinions,* but that doesn't mean she's always right."

"I know." Boy, does he know. "But maybe she's right in a way." With all his time alone lately, he's hoping to at least come out of it as a better version of himself, perhaps slightly more self-aware. Why else has he gone through all of this if not for a tiny bit of growth? But then, he can't picture himself doing anything else, really. Architecture is the only thing he's ever gotten right. His whole life he's been on the outside, needing other people as guideposts for where he belongs. The only time he doesn't is when he's drawing up workable plans for someone's unreasonable and incongruous desire for a traditional colonial with Romanesque interior archways and a Monterey double wraparound porch.

"Do you think I'm making the same mistakes?"

Link's face is drawn, mouth flat. "You're the only person who can answer that, Carter."

Carter frowns.

Link's face softens. "Look, I'm trying to work out the same thing, you know. Where the hell do I go from here?"

Lost together, then. Carter doesn't have answers for Link's future any more than he does for his own. But a small step forward, one week ahead in time, that's not too much. "We could go out?" Carter offers. "Dinner Friday night."

Link sinks onto the couch, tucks up into a ball, and yawns. "Carter Jacob, are you asking me out on a date?"

Carter shrugs. "I guess I am, yeah." They're doing everything out of order or really with no order or sense at all, so why not. "Would you like to go out on a date with me?" Link smiles at him sweetly, and affection rushes through Carter's veins.

"I would love to."

Carter doesn't stay; Link is sleepy, and he's restless. Back at his house, he sands a new spot on the floor. The more he does, the less finished the house seems. Carter's arms hurt, and his eyes are bleary, and he accidentally sands too deeply, possibly damaging the hundred-year-old flooring because he has no idea what he's doing. A YouTube tutorial does not a vintage flooring expert make. Yet he can't make himself stop and go to sleep. He can feel the funnel cloud of panic start to spin at the edge of his mind.

The last time he was with Link the way he was tonight, Carter closed his eyes and went to sleep and when he opened them again, Link was gone. That's his entire problem with art that only exists for itself; it's too fragile. Without meaning and sense to guide him, Carter is trying to steady himself on a pathway made of smoke.

THIRTY-ONE

CARTER SPENDS THE DAYS LEADING up to his date with Link dithering over what to do with the house and dithering over whether or not to accept the job. It takes him four days to decide on a paint color for the living room, and then on the fifth day he swipes one test patch of green onto the wall and does nothing more. Assuming he has other offers and is merely deciding between them instead of being completely incapable of making a decision, the New Orleans firm offers him an even better benefits package. Where is Stan the security guard when Carter needs him?

Thank heavens his clothes all look the same. In a short sleeve button-down and crisp slacks, his hair parted to its usual side, Carter, happy to leave the house and his thoughts behind, goes to the warehouse on Friday. It's oppressively hot and sticky once again, and the wide warehouse doors are pushed open. Massive fans whoosh so loudly Carter's entrance goes unnoticed. Eli and Link are hunched over the table that holds Eli's glassblowing tools and instruments, discussing something in tense, low tones. Eli's eyebrows are furrowed, his head is dropped into both hands, and Link is repeatedly twisting up and loosening their hair.

"Evening," Carter says, announcing his presence. "Everything all right?"

Link hasn't changed out of their welding coveralls, hasn't even undone the top half. Eli is holding a paper down with the flat of his hand; the corners lift one by one in time with the clockwise motion of a nearby fan.

"Carter," Link says, confused, then wide-eyed. "Oh, crap. Carter. I'm so sorry, I got completely sidetracked."

"It's okay," Carter says, relieved that Link didn't forget about him altogether.

"It is not." Link stands, attention still focused on whatever that paper is about. "I'll go change; give me ten minutes." Link's phone rings from inside the front coverall pocket, and whoever is on the other end makes them amend, "Fifteen minutes."

Link takes the stairs two at a time up to the loft while talking on the phone; their voice is completely drowned out by the fans. Carter tries to smooth down his windswept hair, but it's no use. He hasn't talked to Eli much since he become one half of Eli-and-Paige, so Carter says, "It's windy in here," just for something to say.

Eli looks up as if he'd forgotten Carter was there. "What? Oh, yeah. It gets insanely fucking hot in here during the summer."

Between the weather outside and the fact that both of their art forms involve intense heat, Carter can believe it. "Hmm," he says. He tries to fix his hair again. Maybe he should go upstairs. Link didn't invite him up, but Carter could wait by the door while Link gets ready. The loft doesn't have much private space, but then Carter did see *quite a bit* of Link very recently. Eli curses softly, pulling Carter's attention back to the paper Eli is still scowling at.

"Bad news?" Carter guesses. Jury duty? Car recall? Invitation to a destination wedding?

"Yeah," Eli says, folding the paper back along its creases. "The landlord is hiking up the rent, and I don't really see any way out of it."

Carter *hmms*. "Have you asked why?"

"Oh, I know why," Eli says, smacking the folded letter on the table. "When we first set up shop here this warehouse and all the other ones around it were really fucked up after a hurricane and flooding. We got it cheap with an agreement to fix it up, but now that it is fixed up, he wants us out so he can charge more." He holds up the letter. "It's fucking extortion, right?"

Carter opens his mouth to explain that extortion requires the explicit use of force or threat and this guy is just being an asshole by raising the rent so high that they'll have no choice but to leave. But now is maybe not the time. He nods. "Yeah, that's messed up. So, can't you find a different studio space?" Of course, Link lives here as well.

"Easier said than done," Eli replies. "But that's one of the options we're considering, or I'm considering, if Link really does leave."

Carter's head jerks back as if he just walked right into a plate glass window. "Wait. Leave? Link is leaving?" The metal stairs clang with the sound of someone bounding down them, and Link appears, still on the phone and still wearing coveralls. Leaving? Where?

"You should probably talk to them about it," Eli says.

Carter tries to, but Link tugs him forward, tilting the phone up and covering the mouthpiece as they walk to the door. "Let's just go. I need a drink," Link says, then returns to the still-in-progress phone conversation.

Carter drives as Link talks, taking a right out of the gravel lot with no idea where he's going. He didn't pick a place to go and, since Carter doesn't know New Orleans as Link does, he planned on letting them decide. Randomly taking a side road to another side road, he tries to not listen to Link's side of the conversation, but Link groans loudly, exasperated, and says, "Because it's embarrassing! I keep doing this!"

Carter stops at a red light. He glances at Link, who listens to whoever is on the other side of the conversation, then sighs, says okay several times, and hangs up. "Carter, you are getting ready to have the worst date of your entire life," Link says, finally peeling off the coveralls; beneath is a plain, worn, gray T-shirt and baggy nylon shorts. It's the most dressed-down Carter has ever seen Link.

"Not possible. Not when it's with you," Carter says.

Link touches his arm, looking over with a small, shaky smile. "You're so sweet to me, and I do not deserve it." Link pats Carter's arm and says, "Turn left at the next light. I need you to go by my mom's house."

Link guides him southwest, and Carter is a little bummed at the detour, but excited to see where Link's family lives. He imagines something bohemian, an artist commune or another unique space like Link's loft or Eli's vibrant urban apartment.

"Okay, right here," Link says, pointing out the last turn. It's a regular neighborhood with regular houses in standard ranch style with little flat yards. Maybe artist hippie communes look like suburban neighborhoods built in the '80s. They get out of the car, and Link says, "This was my grandmother's place. Danielle was taking care of her for a while, until she moved on. Still strange to see my mom here and not her."

"Oh, gosh," Carter says as they head up the walkway. "I'm so sorry to hear that."

The screen door opens with a screech. "Oh no, she's alive," Link says. "Just in a nursing home. Still as fiery as ever." The wooden door is painted a soft yellow and opens to a woman with round brown eyes, black hair streaked with gray in a thick braid that reaches her waist, and Link's wide, full-lipped smile. She's wearing a billowy shirt splattered in a riot of colors and pants that seem to be constructed from patches and fabric scraps. She welcomes them in with a rich, mellifluous voice.

"Carter, this is Danielle Boudreaux, my mother."

Danielle, Link's mother, moves close to Carter as if she's going to give him a hug, but presses two fingers against his head, right between his eyebrows. She shakes her head and tuts, "Oh, my, your third eye is *completely* closed."

THIRTY-TWO

C~ARTER RUBS AT THE SPOT~ on his forehead where his third eye is apparently in real trouble. "Oh," he says, frowning. "What does that mean?"

"It doesn't mean anything, Carter. Don't worry about it." Link touches his elbow and tugs him back from Danielle's scrutiny.

"Well! Somebody's aura is a dark, angry orange today," Danielle says, with an intent look at Link, while she flutters her hands around the outline of Link's body. Then she smiles. "Hey! Does anyone want some lemonade? I just made a fresh batch!" She sweeps into the house and around a corner, and then Carter hears kitchen things clang and bang and crash.

The house's interior looks like a time capsule, as if it was indeed built in the '80s, decorated and furnished in that decade as well, and then left in that exact state with pastels and floral prints, gold-trimmed glass tables, and oddly shaped mirrors everywhere.

"Carter and I are actually trying to go on date, Danielle," Link calls, "So can we just get to whatever I urgently needed to come here for?"

It brings Carter up short, that Link calls her by her first name, for one, and then the rebuke and the clear voicing of displeasure. Carter knows he and Link had very different upbringings, but the casualness and lack of deference to parental authority is still surprising. When Link was on the phone, Carter assumed the conversation was with a close friend because that was how it sounded: honest, forthcoming. Carter is a grown adult who doesn't do everything his mother says, but when he defies her wishes it's behind her back. He's hidden most of himself and his entire dating life, except Matthew, and that's only because they got engaged and he had no choice. His mother certainly isn't a friend.

Danielle comes out of the kitchen with two glasses and sets them on a coffee table in the living room. There is a stack of money in the center of the table. She taps the bills, then the couch. "Come sit, come sit." Carter does as he's told, and Link reluctantly follows. "I had a booth at this wonderful craft fair last weekend. Did very well. I want you to take some and put it toward your rent. That way you don't have to leave New Orleans if that isn't what you want, though I respect your decision either way."

"You know I don't like taking your money." Link, drink untouched, perches on the edge of the couch.

"And you know that I don't like having too much cash around," Danielle counters. "It's a summoner of evil spirits and dark energies."

Link and Danielle glare at each other with matching stubborn expressions, and Carter, not knowing what else to do, picks up his lemonade. Inside the glass are generous slices of lemon, several large green leaves, and a long sprig of something else green. Carter pokes around with his straw until he finds a clear path to the actual lemonade and takes a sip, then chokes a little on the sour, unsweetened, herbal taste. Link and Danielle turn to look at him.

"That is—" He coughs instead of finishing his sentence, then sets the drink back down. His eyes water a little. "So, you're also an artist?" Carter asks Danielle, trying to steer the conversation into more neutral territory.

She gasps. "I am!" She slides next to him on the couch, touches his head again, and then his chest and stomach and lower back as she says, eyes intense and very close to Carter's, "My medium is the mind and body." She puts both hands on Carter's chest and rubs slow circles around his pectorals.

"Oh," Carter says, wishing he was still choking on his lemon herb water. "Um." As Link's mom continues to rub his chest, Carter looks desperately to Link for help. Link is laughing at him.

"I'm sorry, I told you she was strange."

"Spoken like a true Sagittarius," Danielle says, then flutters her hands around Link's general area again. "Normalcy is an oppressive social construct designed to reinforce the status quo and keep us from fully embracing our own inherent power." She pats Link's cheek, then turns to Carter. "Isn't that right, Carter?"

"I—" Carter starts. Reading people's auras and energies is as ridiculous as believing one's personality is the result of a pattern of stars falling in a certain place at a certain time, yet there is something in the way Danielle is looking at him, as if she knows him. "Right," Carter says, sipping more sour lemonade. It goes down a little easier now that he knows what to expect.

Link sighs, squeezes Danielle's hand, and gathers up the stack of bills. "Okay. Fine. Thanks, I'll pay you back as soon as I can."

"No need," Danielle says, "The universe will pay me back in karma."

"If only my landlord took karma as payment," Link quips. Their phone goes off. "Excuse me. I need to take this."

As soon as Link disappears down the hallway leading to the bedrooms, Danielle also stands, hovers above Carter, and moves her hands in circles over his head. She asks his birthday and seems pleased at the late January date, then says, "May I read your aura, Carter? Your energies are simply fascinating." Carter is unaware of how to how to politely turn down an aura reading, so he agrees.

Danielle instructs him to lie down on the couch. She takes six deep breaths and closes her eyes, then opens them; her gaze has gone unfocused. She seems to be looking off to the side, at the busy floral pattern of the couch beneath him—or beyond him—and moves her hands over Carter's head and the length of his body without making physical contact. She hums in several different intonations: curious, then confused, intrigued, then horrified, then pleased. Finally, she says, "Well. Well, well, well."

Carter sits up as Link comes back down the hallway. Carter's aura must be in even worse condition than his third eye. "What? What is it?"

Danielle sits, palms pressed against her cheeks, her expression serious. "It's just—your primary energy is so yellow, indicating a seeker of truth and joy and knowledge. But it's so clouded with gray I don't know how you haven't gotten lost in it completely." She shakes her head with dismay, then makes a circling motion around Carter's pelvic area. "And there's the whole matter of this purple sexual energy—so *raw*."

"Okay!" Link interrupts. "We're definitely gonna stop talking about that."

"Oh, Link, it's nothing to be uncomfortable about!" Danielle protests, though she moves her hands farther from Carter's lower half. "Sex is—"

"Humanity in its purest form, yeah, yeah," Link intones, stopping a speech they've probably heard many times, then motioning toward a sliding glass door in the dining room. "Carter, could I see you outside for a minute?"

THIRTY-THREE

THERE'S A LITTLE SQUARE PATIO out back, and a small fenced-in yard. Link sits in one of the sun-bleached patio chairs, and Carter sits in the other one. "Was it Eli?" Carter asks, after Link only offers thoughtful silence. "Any news about the warehouse?"

"No," Link says, plucking at a broken piece of wicker on the chair as they scan the backyard. "You know, I didn't as spend much time here as I wish I had, as a kid. I didn't really spend much time anywhere." Link looks over to Carter, then quickly away; they seem unable to look him in the eye. Whatever that phone call was about, it changed things. Carter braces himself for what's inevitably coming.

"I came back to New Orleans because I wanted stability. I wanted commitment and roots and I... I think now it's just not meant to be." Link twists the piece of wicker until it breaks off. "Do you understand what I'm trying to say, Carter?"

Along the back fence is a cluster of dandelions, some yellow, some with white fluffy seeds, ready to spread the invasive weed elsewhere. Contrary to popular opinion, what qualifies as a weed isn't a matter of perspective, but an actual classification of plant characteristics, tenacity chief among them; an ability to grow and thrive anywhere. Carter is not a dandelion.

"Things are not 'meant to be,'" Carter says, once he can trust his voice to remain steady. "They either are, or they aren't." He swallows hard and turns to face Link. "You either do or you don't. We make choices. The whims of the universe have nothing to do with it."

After a moment, Link meets his eyes. "That's fair."

After everything he went through with Matthew and everything that happened with him and Link before, Carter would just rather know that it's over than remain suspended in uncertainty, hoping for the best. Carter states plainly, because he knows no other way of saying it or hiding the truth of it, "I want to be with you."

Link nods. "Me too." Carter breathes out a sigh of relief that doesn't even last until the next breath in. "But," Link says. "It's like we keep getting close, but not quite. The timing is never quite right. Carter, I might be leaving soon…"

Carter starts to tell Link that it doesn't matter, that he'll be with Link wherever, just say the word. But that would be making the same mistake, relying on someone else to define his life for him again, acting on a fear of being alone again, and he can't. "Do you think we'll ever get the timing right?" he asks.

Link's eyes search Carter's face. "I hope so."

Carter crosses his legs and tilts his face up to the sun. He shoos a bug away. "Where do you think you might end up?"

The bug zigzags to Link, who watches it come close and then zoom off. "I have some possibilities in New York, maybe Chicago. Seattle."

The irony of Link potentially ending up in Chicago after Carter left that area to be here is not lost on Carter. He could go back easily enough; there isn't much tying him to New Orleans. He probably won't. Carter didn't come here for Link, not on purpose, and he shouldn't leave for Link, either. Is this their story, then, he and Link? A series of endings?

"I could wait for you," Carter offers. It sounds like a question. Link shakes their head.

"I watched her wait. Danielle. Like she had to put her life on permanent hold until my father was ready, and he never was. I swore I wouldn't be like that but—" Link shrugs. "Here we are. Relationships and family were just never the priority."

Carter rolls his head to one side. "Because Chumbawumba was?"

A wide smile breaks across Link's face. "Because Chumbawumba was. Yep." Link reaches over and taps Carter's knee. "For the record, I'd rather not go."

"Okay," Carter says. He believes it. It still hurts.

"And, Carter, you are… so sweet and smart and funny and interesting and *sincere*." Link smiles at him, though their eyes are sad. "You deserve a solid foundation and a full life with someone who has their shit figured out. I don't want you to wait around for me, okay?"

Carter nods at the ground. "Sure."

"Carter." Link squeezes his knee. "Please?"

Carter has to count seventy-three patio tiles before he can push his feelings away and speak. "Okay," he says. "I won't."

Danielle chooses that moment to push the sliding glass door open. "Oh, Carter! Have you ever tried cupping? Because I would love to see if we can get your qi flowing!"

Carter doesn't want to stick around and find out what that is. "I should, um." He stands, shoving his hands in his pockets. "I have so much to do on my house still."

"Carter is fixing up an old house over near Lakewood," Link says, voice lilting in a fake-cheery way. "It's something he's wanted to do for a long time."

Of course Link remembers the conversation at the diner about Carter's dream of fixing up an old house, and of course, Link is looking at him with admiration and encouragement even now, at another ending. "Yes. It's a camelback style built in—"

"I have just the thing!" Danielle snaps her fingers and disappears into the house. Link follows her. Still not knowing what else to do, Carter follows too.

Danielle roots around in a kitchen cabinet and pulls down clear jars full of green leafy things and green powdery things and brown seed things and colorful dried flowers. Then, from the windowsill, she removes a ceramic jar, pulls the cork stopper, and shakes into it whatever herbs and plants she brought down. "Link made this." She shakes the ceramic jar; it's lumpy and misshapen, collapsed a bit in the center.

"Ceramics are not my forte," Link says, cringing. "It was a phase, really."

"Confused, huh?" Carter says.

Link smiles. Even now it's impossible to not be what he and Link have always been: connected, easy. The joyful spark catches in Carter's chest every time. "I was, yeah. But I'm not anymore, don't worry."

And even now, as always, Carter wants to kiss Link more than he's ever wanted anything.

"Okay!" Danielle says, dramatically popping the cork back in the jar. "Unfortunately, I am fresh out of marjoram, but not to worry, I put star anise in there instead." She hands him the jar, grinning hopefully.

"Oh," Carter says. "Um. Thank you." He looks to Link, who once again just seems amused.

"It's for good luck and protection in your new home," Danielle explains. That's a relief; Carter was worried he might have to smoke it or perform a ritual of some sort. Danielle places her hands around Carter's hands on the jar. "Sage, cornflowers, hyssop, lavender, lemongrass, honeysuckle, and Sampson snakeroot, of course."

"Of course," Carter agrees.

She closes her eyes, and Link does too. As Danielle begins to speak, Link's lips move. "Cleanse this space; remove the past. You'll find your happiness at long last. Fill this space with joy and love, sending healing from above."

Carter is too mystified to do anything but stare at the jar in stunned silence. Magic spells are as ridiculous as… well, *magic spells.* Yet somehow, in this kitchen, with Danielle's sure hands on his, her soothing voice wishing him happiness at long last, with Link's presence, even with Link leaving, even with Carter agreeing to move on, Carter feels something like peace settle his shoulders and stitch through his heart. Danielle opens the jar and tilts it toward Carter's nose. He takes a deep breath.

When Carter gets back home, he places the jar in the center of his dining room table and opens the email he's been putting off answering.

To: Regina Marshall-Yu
From: Carter J. Jacob
Subject: re: Magnolia Modern Architectural Group - Employment

Dear Regina,

After meeting with you in person and carefully reviewing the position offered to me via email, I would like to formally accept the offer as is outlined in the second correspondence email that was sent to me on Monday, May the Fifth. I look forward to starting employment on the first of next month, as was previously discussed in the initial email...

Carter stops, squints at the email and backspaces. There's formal and then there's "I'll be bringing my perfectly portioned, nutritionally balanced lunch to work in a bento box and leaving at five-thirty sharp with no fraternizing whatsoever," formal.

Dear Regina,

Thank you so much for the opportunity to work at Magnolia Modern. The work your firm does is an inspiring combination of traditional design and modern architectural movements that I would be thrilled to join. I'd like to come by on Monday morning and work out the details of my start date and position, if this works with your schedule. I look forward to working with you and the rest of the firm.

Best regards,
Carter J. Jacob

It's not his dream job, perhaps, but that was never the shape of his dreams anyway. Carter drifts off to sleep, noticing for the first time how loud the cicadas and crickets are here, and how, if he moves his sleeping bag to the other side of the room, he can sleep beneath the steady glow of the moon.

THIRTY-FOUR

CARTER'S NEW OFFICE IS IN a newly built home in a newly built neighborhood; the rooms inside are laid out in office suites instead of living spaces. The effect is faux-homey, but Carter appreciates the comfortable design aesthetic they were going for. On his first day, he learns that the initial team-client meetings to suss out exactly what they want in a home are handled by a customer liaison, and that's his least favorite part of the job passed right along to someone else. On his second day, Carter is carefully looking over his HR packet near quitting time when another production architect stops by his office.

"Hey, man, a bunch of us in the office get dinner together on Tuesdays; you in?"

Carter struggles to remember his name. He's been trying to use word association to help him remember people here. Jeremy, that was it. Carter starts to beg off with his usual excuses, the same ones he used in Aurora to keep to himself: he's not really hungry, he's fine, actually he's heading out now, he wouldn't want to intrude on an established friend group. He's boring anyway. But he has flooring contractors at his house, and he was planning to eat out tonight; might as well go with other people. He told Link he would.

"Yeah, that sounds great," Carter says. Jeremy raps on the door frame twice, then shoots Carter finger guns before leaving. *Finger Gun Jeremy*, Carter thinks with a smile. He seems okay, otherwise.

They go to a sports bar: Finger Gun Jeremy, Sara Without an H, Tom from Tulsa, Tall Chris, Short Chris, Pilar who drives a Prius, Too Many Plants in His Office Isaiah, and him. Regular Old Carter. There's a soccer game on TV, a sport for which Carter sat on the bench enough as a kid to follow along now and make passable sport-related conversation. Pilar asks him how he's liking New Orleans. Jeremy knows a family from Aurora, so they play the "do you know…" game for a while, and everyone is really interested in his house. He gets to talk about stylistic embellishments verses purely utilitarian facades for historical shotgun houses for quite some time with people who have an opinion on that sort of thing. It's not the same as Link's sweetly enamored interest, but it's nice. Sara gives him the card of a local restoration contractor who specializes in historic dwellings and has helped rebuild the parts of lower New Orleans that were hardest hit by recent flooding.

"Thanks," Carter says.

"Of course." Sara Without an H is from Wisconsin, it turns out, and came to New Orleans in search of a place with a little more character and a little more warmth, just as he did. "We get together to play pool usually twice a month, too, if you're interested." Sara says. He is interested.

On Friday after his second week at his new job, Carter goes home to glossy, impeccably restored wood floors. The one camping chair in the living room and the other pushed up to the dining table that Link made look particularly sad now, but he promised he'd wait and go furniture shopping with Paige. Except for Tuesdays and Friday night pizza, Carter has been cooking at home, and on Sunday he has a catfish fillet with greens sizzling in a new cast iron pan when he gets a text from Link. It's the first he's heard from them since that day at Danielle's.

Link: *We're out studio hunting. I saw this and thought of you.*

It's a photo of a white sign with bold red lettering advertising a real estate company, with little placards hanging below the sign that announce: APARTMENT. COMMERCIAL. HAUNTED.

Carter leaves his finished dinner to warm on the stove as he quickly texts back: *Gimmick*

Link: *Such a cynic Carter Jacob*
Carter: *Just pragmatic is all*
Link: *I know this. It's adorable. Usually.*

In his kitchen, alone, Carter smiles and writes, *Hey I did let Danielle read my aura.*

Link: *And did you believe her?*

Carter: *No. Well, the part about my raw sexual energy was right on. Oh wow, do you think your mom is into me?*

Link doesn't text back, and Carter is worried he crossed a line. He plates his dinner and grabs a sparkling water from the new fridge, sits down in the camping chair at the table, and eats his dinner for one. Finally, Link sends another message.

Link: *OMG I was laughing so hard I had to excuse myself from the tour. The realtor probably thinks I've lost it.*

Carter: *Haha. How is the search going by the way?*

Link: *Still haven't found anything we can afford but Eli is optimistic*

Carter: *And you?*

Link: *I've been in touch with some folks in Seattle. It's Plan B for now.*

As much as he is trying to build a life for himself, by himself, Carter really doesn't want Link to go. He still can't imagine a future that doesn't involve Link in some way.

Carter: *I don't think Seattle is haunted at all, just saying*

Link: *Are you kidding? That whole city is an eldritch horror unto itself*

Carter: *Never been*

Link: *Gasp! Well if I end up there you'll just have to come visit right away :)*

It sets Carter at ease, the notion that perhaps he and Link aren't different planets orbiting the same sun in lonely, singular paths, never to meet, never to line up quite right. Their paths are connected, he's sure of it, just in different places along the way.

Carter: *I'd love that*

Link: *:)*

After his third Tuesday coworker dinner and first pool night, Jeremy stops by his office as Carter is fiddling with a digital blueprint, cranes around the doorjamb, and aims a quick finger-gun-shot in his direction.

"Hey, man, you're gay, right?"

Carter swallows the instinctive fear-then-irritation response to that question, going with a noncommittal, "Sort of."

"Cool, so my cousin is in new in town and he's gay too. I thought maybe you could show him around?" Jeremy's ties are always crooked, Carter has realized. He should have remembered him as Crooked Tie Jeremy.

"Uh. I don't really—" Carter starts. He's not looking to date and particularly isn't looking to be set up by coworkers that he only sort of likes.

"Just casual!" Jeremy protests. "He's lonely. Needs a friend. That's all."

Carter's distracted enough by Jeremy to screw something up in the rendering program, so he scraps the blueprint to start all over. It hasn't been long at all since Carter was new in town and lonely, even when surrounded by people. "Yeah, okay," he says. Jeremy finger-guns at him again and leaves. Carter *really* hopes that is not a family trait.

Evan turns out to be soft-spoken and polite, with dark hair and blue eyes and nervous hands that never keep still. He doesn't really like the club scene, Evan says, and tends to keep to himself, reading or going to museums. He ended up in New Orleans on a job transfer a few months ago. "Jeremy says you were transferred here, too?"

"Not exactly," Carter says, cutting his steak into very small bites.

Evan shakes his head. "I hope he wasn't too annoying when he asked you do this."

Carter shrugs. "No more than usual."

Evan laughs, then blushes and turns his wine glass around and around, staring at the clear stem as he says softly, "I hope this isn't too forward, but I think you're really cute."

"Oh." Carter desperately tries to swallow a gristly bite of steak. "Um. Thanks."

He and Link are not in a relationship. They aren't even in a not-relationship or a fake relationship. Carter should date; he told Link he would. He should be responding to the perfectly nice, good-looking guy who thinks he's really cute. All he can think about is Link and the way Link calls Carter cute, their voice lilting on the *U* as their eyelids lower and flutter, how their wide, full mouth curls into a smile.

Carter awkwardly avoids eye contact with Evan and flags down a waiter. "Two more glasses of wine, please." And then to Evan, changing the topic, "So, Pensacola! What's it like? I've never been."

He cannot imagine that he ever will be.

Link sends him a message after he gets home and changes into pajamas, when he's lying in his new bed staring up at the waning moon.

Heard you were on a date.

Carter grits his teeth and texts back: *Why does Paige feel the need to broadcast my life to the world?*

Link: *Because she's Paige, duh*

Carter: *Right. Well, it wasn't really a date. It wasn't supposed to be anyway.*

Link: *Doesn't answer my question sweetie*

Carter hesitates, wanting to reply that he would have rather been with Link. He finally replies with a not-untruth: *It was fine*

Link: *That's Carter-speak for it was terrible and I was miserable*

Carter: *Yeah, well.*

He smiles to himself; Link really has cracked his code. It wasn't terrible though, just—meh. Minutes pass, and Carter assumes that's the end of the conversation, so he puts his phone face down on his new nightstand and turns off the new lamp. Carter rolls onto his back again, and the phone lights up with another message.

Link: *Is it unfair of me if I say that I'm glad it didn't go well?*

Carter doesn't have to think twice about typing a simple: *No.*

THIRTY-FIVE

Evan comes to the next pool night, arriving with Jeremy, and stands by Carter's side as he racks pool balls. Cues in hand, Short Chris and Tall Chris lean against the other end.

"Need a partner?" Evan asks, voice quietly hesitating, hands wringing on a cue.

"Uh," Carter says. Why is he so bad at this? Has dating always been this hard, or is he just out of practice? Or is *he* always like this? Evan is sweet and still likes him for some reason. "Yeah," Carter says. "I do need a partner, actually."

Chris and Chris make a good team; Carter knows from experience. He beat them once, with Sara, and that's only because Sara is really good and too nice to point out that she could have beaten them without Carter's help. He and Evan do not make a good team.

"Eight ball, corner pocket," Tall Chris calls out, and sinks it.

"Oh, well," Evan says. He wraps both hands tightly around his pool cue, then sets his cheek against it to smile up at Carter. "So I really want to check out the botanical gardens here, and I thought we—"

"You know who would love that?" Carter blurts, backing away with a sudden urge to flee. "Isaiah. He *loves* plants." Carter calls Isaiah over and excuses himself to the bathroom. He locks himself in a stall, rubs his hands over his face, and smooths down his hair. Seriously, what is wrong with him? Evan is—Evan is really—

Evan is not Link.

He is supposed to be working on *not* being hung up on Link, not looking to them for guidance, not waiting around. He has to make his own way, he knows that. If only he could stop thinking about Link *constantly.* And the hardest part is that it's different from when things were over with Matthew. That was lingering resentment and the fear of being alone, the fear of never being enough on his own. That's not what this is at all. Carter just misses Link. Everything is better when Link is around.

Carter groans, the agonized sound echoes across the bathroom, and he realizes too late that he isn't alone in here. He hustles out, irritated at himself, and goes back to talk to Evan. He can go to a botanical garden; it's not as though he'd be promising a lifelong commitment to someone he doesn't have strong feelings for—again. But when he gets back to the section of the bar where the pool tables are laid out, Evan and Isaiah are still deep in conversation, drinking matching drinks, leaning close together, and laughing. That is not what Carter intended to happen, though it does let him off the hook.

Carter plays a few rounds of darts with Pilar, Tom, and Jeremy, then begs off for the evening, saying he has painters coming early in the morning and needs to get to bed, which is true. He doesn't say that he'll have a hard time falling asleep tonight because he needs to wallow for a while. When Carter leaves, Isaiah and Evan are still talking to each other. Walking down the street to where he parked, Carter can't understand why that bothers him so much.

He has to hang out at Paige's apartment all of the following weekend while his house finally gets fresh coats of paint inside and out, until she asks him one too many times what his problem is and then gets angry when he says he's fine. Then he takes his laptop to the park near his house and sits roasting in the sun.

Back at work, Carter is assigned to a new project: an eco-friendly, energy-efficient, modern off-grid home. It's a perfect distraction, so he stays late and goes in early, skips lunches and Tuesday coworker dinners to stay hunkered down in his office. The client wants the home to blend seamlessly into nature but with high-performance modern technology, and the lead architect has some rather lofty ideas of how to make that happen. Actually, making it all happen is challenging in a good way, and Carter can't help but think this sort of thing would be right up Link's alley. The client even wants a sculpture garden in their natural, native-plant-filled yard. He sends a quick email with Link's professional contact information to Pilar, who handles landscape architecture for the firm.

"Yo!" Jeremy's round face and crooked tie appear in Carter's doorway.

"Yes, I know there's cake in the break room," Carter says, not looking up from his work. "Yes, you can have my slice."

"Sweet," Jeremy says. "But actually I wanted to thank you for setting my cousin up with Isaiah. I got my weekends back now. I mean, I love the guy, but his wingman game was some weak sauce."

Carter attempts something akin to a smile. "Great."

"And dude," Jeremy continues, clearly not getting the hint. "I didn't even think about Isaiah, because he had a girlfriend for a while, but it turns out he's *bisexual*. Crazy, right?"

Carter presses his hands together and sets them against the strained line of his mouth, barely keeping his irritation in check. "So crazy," he says. "So, so crazy."

Jeremy finger-guns at him with both hands. "Okay, I'm gonna go eat your cake. Peace."

All along, Cupid has been a tragic figure, Carter thinks. He seems happy, sure, shooting love arrows, bringing connected souls together, an icon of true love. But Cupid is always alone. Cupid is cursed to an eternity of watching other people fall in love, finding their happily ever after. And what does he get for it? Wings? The freedom of flight cannot be worth it.

Carter works on the modern eco-house at home and continues to stay holed up in his office during the day. He ignores calls from his mother and from Paige insisting that she's taking him out to brunch. He even ignores some texts from Link; nothing important, just little funny or interesting things from day to day life. Carter has picked up his phone so many times when he thought, *Oh Link would like this,* or,

I have to tell Link about this. But that's not what they are to each other, so he doesn't.

Carter emerges from his office one afternoon to quickly refill his coffee. He makes brief conversation with Sara about a show they both watch while he stirs in cream and sugar, then goes right back to his office—where he finds Link, dressed in a business-casual look of fitted slacks and a button-down, one bracelet, and one necklace. Their hair is tied back and a subtle, smoky gray lines their eyes.

"Oh," Carter says, discombobulated. Was he thinking about Link so hard he somehow made them materialize out of thin air?

"I was here meeting with Pilar. About the sculptures?"

"Oh!" Carter sets his coffee down, sits, and smooths his tie. "Yes, that's right."

"Thanks for recommending me, by the way." Link sits on the wingback chair in the corner that Carter never uses. Sometimes he'll put a folder on it. "I may be able to afford my rent for another month now."

"Yeah, well. You're amaz—" Carter pauses. Too much. He recalibrates. "I, um, felt that your sculptures would be appropriate for the particular aesthetic we're going for. So."

Link's legs cross and uncross; their hands are set primly on their knees. "Yes. I agree."

Carter makes a popping sound with his mouth. He scratches at his ear.

Link sighs. "This is weird. Why are we being weird?"

It's because I want to kiss you and I can't, Carter thinks, but he says, "I dunno." Carter's eyes stray to his computer; burying himself in work is much easier than this.

"Working on anything fun?" Link says, shoulders lifting, in the relaxed, kind-of-flirty tone Carter is more used to. Carter turns the computer screen so Link can see.

"So the idea is to give the entire home an indoor-outdoor feel. Starting with the all-weather patio that surrounds the entire space, then on into the entryway which will be entirely enclosed in glass, and right next to that will be a living green roof; thus the space offers a panoramic view of vegetation, including vines that will hang down over the glass. Now, it's an open floor plan, but with a different approach to flow and negative space…"

Link lets him ramble on for way too long, until Carter forgets that things are awkward with them and Carter says without thinking, "And here will be a built-in, two-person, cedar-plank soaking tub, which I am definitely getting for my house for reasons I'm *sure* you can imagine." It does not sound kind of flirty; it sounds very blatantly like a come-on. Carter backtracks quickly with a fake laugh, adding, "You know, for when I have a date that does go well."

"Right, yeah." Link nods, too rapidly, then stands and strides quickly to the door. "Well, I'll leave you to it. Um, bye."

Carter drops back in his chair and covers his face with both hands. *Dammit.*

THIRTY-SIX

"BRUNCH TIME!"

Carter is in his rattiest pajamas; his face is covered in itchy stubble, and his hair is uncombed. "I don't want brunch," he says, squinting angrily into the morning sun. He spent all last night and most of the early morning battling wallpaper in the dining room, the last room with unfinished walls. The wallpaper defeated him. He's hit a new low.

Paige waves him off. "Yes, you do."

He does; she's right. He just doesn't want to leave the house right now, possibly ever. "Just bring me back a spinach omelet, side of bacon, hash browns, and a few mimosas," Carter says, closing the front door.

Paige slams her entire body into the door. It springs wide open again. "I'm not a delivery person, Carter. Go change. What is this?" She gestures at his hair and face and all the rest of him. "You look gross."

"You're always good for an ego boost, Paige." He sits in his living room camping chair. The house is really coming along, renovation-wise, but he still has hardly any furniture, other than the new bed, which he barely slept in last night. They were supposed to go furniture shopping today after brunch. Carter just doesn't care anymore.

"I am, aren't I?" Paige says, smiling fake-sweetly. "You also smell bad."

Carter does take a shower and shave and change, not because he admits that he wants to go to brunch and *not* because Paige told him to, but because he did smell bad, a little.

She drags him to a small café near the river where they're seated on a brick patio overlooking Canal Street. Large, lazy fans rotate overhead, and the tables around them buzz with quiet morning conversations as cars pass on the street. Carter, needing something less effervescent than a mimosa today, orders a Bloody Mary.

"I have almost enough artists committed; we just need to decide if it's still too hot to have the event outdoors at the warehouse, or if we need to clear out the inside somehow," Paige sips a ruby sunrise as she fills Carter in on an event she's planning to help Eli and Link raise some money.

"Doesn't really solve the long-term issue," Carter points out. Not wanting to be negative, but—no, maybe he *does* want to be negative.

"No, but at least I'm doing something," Paige mutters.

Carter sets his drink down. "And what is that supposed to mean?"

Paige opens her mouth, then takes a breath and closes it. "Nothing, never mind." She taps her finger on the table, then says, "Ooh, gossip! Meredith and Malcolm totally hit it off at the party." *Of course they did.*

Carter glowers at Paige's excited face until her expression is closer to his own. They order, shrimp and grits for him, bananas Foster pancakes for Paige, then sit quietly. The table next to theirs has a dog tied underneath it, a big fluffy dog of some indiscernible breed. It sits watching the steamy New Orleans Sunday morning go by, completely content. The thick fog surrounding Carter lifts a bit.

"Sorry, I haven't been sleeping well," Carter says. He had his broken heart re-broken, can't figure out how to be around Link again, sucks at dating, and is incapable of hanging wallpaper. "I guess I'm just in a mood."

"Yeah, I noticed," Paige bites back, then winces at her own tone. "Sorry."

Carter chuckles. "We are not great at being nice to each other."

"No," Paige laughs. "You know, speaking of that, I've been wanting to tell you that I'm proud of you." Carter stares blankly. Never once in his life has she said that, or implied it, or acted in a manner that would suggest she approves of anything he's ever done. Paige continues, "Yeah,

I mean. Your house isn't a total dump anymore. You got a good job that isn't making you dead inside. You aren't a total pathetic shut-in lately, besides the last of couple weeks, I mean."

"Thanks." Carter takes a drink of his Bloody Mary. "I think."

"You haven't even mentioned Matthew in a while."

Their food comes, interrupting the conversation. He hasn't thought about Matthew much lately, it's true, but he never talked to Paige about him unless he was feeling particularly weak and upset, so it isn't as if they've had tons of conversations about him. Paige has never been shy about her dislike for his ex.

"I'm sure not hearing about him must be a relief for you," Carter says, stabbing a shrimp with his fork; the grumpy gray fog threatens to fall back around him.

"It is," Paige says around a bite of pancake and flambéed banana. "You know why?"

Of course he knows why. "Because it was an uncomfortable reminder of my identity and sexuality?" She's trying to be better now, and she is, but that doesn't erase the years he spent being judged and dismissed and penalized for being himself.

Paige sets her fork down and leans closer over the table. "Hey, remember when you were like, thirteen and obsessed with *The Princess Bride*?"

"I remember you broke the DVD on purpose," Carter says. And he remembers the massive crushes he had on both Cary Elwes and Robin Wright.

"After the one hundredth viewing in a row I couldn't take it anymore," Paige protests. "I was also fifteen and a huge jerk. *Anyway*, I watched a few times, even though I acted like I hated it. And I remember thinking… the way that Westley looked at Buttercup, you know? Like, even when she was ordering him around and stuff? I wanted that."

Carter quietly considers this. Her dating history seems to say otherwise, but she was never serious with any of those guys, not the way she is with Eli. "I guess I did too," Carter admits. "It's just a movie, though. A goofy one."

Paige stabs more pancake and bananas onto her fork. "Maybe. But if I can't get someone who looks at me like Westley, for real, then I swore I would at least never be like our parents."

Carter lifts his chin. "You mean how Dad looks at Mom like she's a stranger?"

"And Mom looks at Dad like she wants to kill him, but he isn't worth the trouble?" Paige adds. "Exactly."

Carter takes a bite, chews, swallows, then asks, "What does that have to do with you hating Matthew from the moment you met him, though?" He and Matthew weren't Buttercup and Westley, sure, but they weren't Carter's parents either. Things weren't that bad, especially not in the beginning, when they were better at pretending.

Paige shrugs. "I didn't like the way he looked at you."

After brunch, they stroll to a nearby furniture boutique, as Paige is newly committed to local artisans and this happens to be a store to which she sells art pieces. They're shown around by the shop owner, which is a nice perk. The tufted blue velvet dining chairs and hand-carved reclaimed wood sideboard Paige and the owner help him pick out are exceptionally gorgeous, and outrageously expensive.

"This is the rest of my entire furniture budget," Carter says as they oversee the delivery at Carter's house.

"Ask Link to make you something." Paige directs a delivery person to the dining room.

"Link doesn't want me to bother them," Carter says.

"Carter, you are so clueless." Paige rolls her eyes and shakes her head. The chairs and sideboard are set up in the dining room, and Paige barks at Carter, "Bring the table back here."

Carter obediently goes to the front room to fetch the table, but *only* because he wants to. It's heavy; heavier than Carter remembers. Afraid to scuff his newly refinished floors by dragging it through the house, Carter tips the table onto its side to roll it through.

"I don't know how Link carried this thing down the street alone." Carter leaves the table on its side as he catches his breath while bracing himself on the bottom "trunk" part.

"It's because you're a weakling," Paige says, an offhand insult without any real heat.

Carter ignores her when he'd usually insult her back, because something on the underside of the table's metal trunk has caught his eye. Carter moves around it, crouching down and brushing his fingers along the center. It's a flower made of glass, set to one side of a disk that makes up the table's base. Either he's seeing things he wants to see, or Link intentionally hid a flower that looks just like the one Carter picked on that picnic, on the first day he and Link spent together.

THIRTY-SEVEN

THE DAY OF THE ART bazaar to save the warehouse comes at a not-great time for Carter. He made plans a while ago with Sara and her wife, for one, and there's a construction crew taking over his house, for two. He's also juggling multiple projects at work and avoiding his mother's increasingly frequent phone calls.

She calls again early that afternoon, when he's trying to eat a sandwich surrounded by the ambiance of drills and hammers and construction workers shouting at each other. He takes the phone and half a turkey sandwich outside. His lawn is still a scrabbly stretch of dirt with a few sad tufts of grass. Pilar has drawn up some suggestions for him, but they're waiting until the heat backs off a little before they get started. Carter waves to his neighbor next door, who is working in his garden and calls over that he has more peppers and tomatoes for Carter. Carter's neighbor in the back is watching her kids play in the yard, and Carter tosses a stray ball back over and chats for a minute. Other the other side is an older, long-married couple; Carter makes a mental note to bring their trash and recycling cans up later and return the pie pan he borrowed.

Finally, with nothing left to distract him, Carter rests against the back wall under a slight shadow from the roof and calls his mother back while construction workers stomp overhead. The phone call starts the way all their conversations go.

"Hello, Mother," Carter says.

"Hello," his mother says.

"How are you?" Carter asks.

"Fine and you?"

"Fine as well." Whether it's true or not, it doesn't matter. "How's Dad?"

"Your father is fine."

And then she'll usually guilt him for not calling some family member he's never been close to and mention someone's daughter who is "such a lovely girl, Carter" and talk about something they're fixing on the house or a recent antique store find or a restaurant she's been to and none of it ever goes beyond surface level unless she's telling Carter how he's disappointed her this time. She surprises him, though.

"Your house is really coming along."

How did she…? Paige. "Yeah, it's getting there."

"Well, I admit that I never expected this foolish New Orleans whimsy to actually work out for either of you. Consider me pleased to have been mistaken." She says New Orleans strangely, with a harsh *O* and long *E*.

Carter is so taken aback by her approval, though reluctant and backhanded, that he answers honestly, "I wasn't sure if it would work either. I've been a little lost since Ma—" He stops cold; his mother can't even stand him saying Matthew's name, and not for the reasons Paige claims. She's made her position on that very clear. She'll dismiss his heartbreak and loneliness as the result of his own choice to make his life needlessly difficult. "I've been a tad rootless, lately," Carter says.

"Well, I can certainly relate to that," his mother replies, surprising him with her candor once again. Maybe it took this distance between them to gain a little understanding. "You know, I only want your and Paige's happiness and success, Carter."

The familiar statement doesn't feel like barbwire wrapping his throat, as it usually does. "I know," Carter says.

The Art Bazaar and Benefit is being held in the same empty gravel lot next to the warehouse where Paige's party was held. This is a much more subdued affair; it's quiet when Carter approaches, with no cupcakes in hand this time. There are card tables laid out in rows, with a wide variety of art for sale, from paintings to pottery to jewelry to cartoon portraits. Link has a table at the far end of the second row, and Eli is right in the front. There's good turnout of people perusing the tables.

"Carter!" Eli calls. "Hope you brought money."

"Ha, I did. Yep." He shakes Eli's hand. "This is pretty impressive."

"It's all Paige," Eli says, tugging the bill of his hat down to block the harsh sun as one of the few puffy white clouds in the sky drifts away. "Wish the weather had been nicer. At least it's not raining, right?"

"Yeah." Carter shades his eyes with his hand. He should have kept his sunglasses on. "So is this gonna work, do you think?"

"Long-term?" Eli says. "No. And honestly, Link already has one foot out the door. One and a half, even. But I wouldn't put it past Paige to do one of these every month if she has to."

Carter spots Paige, waving her hands wildly as she bosses someone around; they look as though they have food for sale, but nowhere to set it up.

"She is a force to be reckoned with."

"Yes, she is," Eli says in a tone that makes Carter turn back around. Eli is watching Paige too. Suddenly Carter understands, what Paige meant by not liking the way Matthew looked at him. It was never, ever anything close to the raw adoration in Eli's gaze.

Paige comes rushing over, pointing at Carter and then at Eli. "Carter, go buy something. Eli, I need you to find a table or something for these *idiots* who can't read *instructions*. 'Bring your own table.' It could not be clearer." Paige throws her hands up in frustration and starts to rush off again, but not before Eli says, "As you wish."

Paige smiles and winks at him as she goes.

Eli comes around the table, gives Carter a friendly pat on the arm, and thanks him for coming. Carter has no clue how to be a protective brother and is not great at being macho or aggressive. And Paige is really the last person who needs protection, anyway. He doesn't know what else to say, though, to thank Eli for caring about Paige the way he does, for making her happy the way he has. Carter is jealous of the way they found each other and found a way to fit together so easily. Mostly, though, he's happy for them, really and truly.

Carter grabs Eli by the arm and says, in what is probably the least threatening tone of voice ever, "If you hurt my sister, I'll kick your ass."

Eli smiles, then forces his face into a semi-serious expression. "Got it." Carter releases his arm so he can go. "Thanks, Carter."

Carter walks around; he can't stay long. He buys a painting of an evening landscape from Malcolm; the blues and grays will go perfectly in his dining room, with the wallpaper he paid someone else to put up. He buys sunglasses, too; though the bedazzled frames aren't exactly his style, he's tired of squinting.

"Hi!"

He's finally meandered to Link's station. "Hi," he says, then scans the table and taps two of those cool metal plants Link had at the Saturday market, back when Carter made a fool of himself. One of many times, it seems. "I'll take two of these, please."

"Oh, okay." Link takes the sculptures Carter pointed out and starts to wrap them in paper. "Hey, so. If you want, we can hang out after. Play cards, or maybe get something to eat." Link can't seem to focus on wrapping the plants and looks up at Carter.

"I have plans, actually. With Sara, from work."

"Oh, yeah. Okay." Link looks down, biting their lip and hurriedly wrapping. "That's great for you. Yeah. Where, uh. Where're you going?"

"Funny enough, we're doing that same Garden District tour that was rained out when you and I tried to go. I finally get to go into some of those amazing old mansions."

Link harshly yanks off a strip of tape. The dispenser falls sideways. Packages wrapped, Link hands over the two metal plants and says, in a flat, wistful voice. "Kind of ironic that we couldn't do the one thing you actually would have been interested in that week, huh?"

"I was interested in stuff," Carter says.

"You were sweet enough to pretend you were," Link replies.

Carter tucks the two packages under one arm and the painting under the other and thinks back to that week he and Link spent together. He remembers having fun doing whatever Link wanted because he was so awed by New Orleans and awed by Link that everything was cast in a rosy glow. He can't say that kind of stuff anymore, though; Link wouldn't want him to.

"I liked the food," Carter says. He did. He still does. "And, oh, the picnic. Or, I guess that's still food-related."

Link's gaze intensifies, as though they're trying to see behind Carter's sunglasses to his eyes, trying to read something there. Is it about the picnic? That flower? Should Carter say something about it? Then someone crosses in front of Carter to look at Link's art pieces and the moment is gone.

"See you soon," Carter says, not knowing if he will. "Good luck in Seattle, if I don't see you." Link's head bows, and Carter turns away.

The Garden District Tour is great, or it would be if Carter's attention wasn't so split the whole time. He's glad Sara has her wife along for company, because Carter is a terrible companion for the whole tour and dinner. At home, he has to sign off on the day's work with the foreman and he barely even gives the repairs a cursory glance of approval.

Nothing he does about Link feels right except for just *being* with Link. Something that should be so simple has always been so complicated. Now Link is leaving, to move across the country. Even if Carter knew what do, it's too late.

"Will you be renting the property?" the foreman asks, flipping to another form on his clipboard.

Carter shakes his head. "No, I'm the primary resident."

The foreman flips the papers back. "Okay, good. There's an extra inspection process we have to go through for rentals in this county; they've really cracked down lately. Landlords not in compliance get hit with steep penalties. Some of the repeat offenders have even gone to the slammer."

Carter's head tilts; his attention is piqued. "Can you explain the details of this extra inspection process to me? In the event that I do rent it someday."

THIRTY-EIGHT

New Orleans City Hall is a giant, white rectangular building with row after row of narrow mirrored windows; it's disappointing, architecturally speaking, but Carter supposes that it certainly fulfills the "form follows function" ethos. He takes a very plain elevator up to the very plain seventh floor, where he's directed to a suite, where he's directed to a desk, where the city clerk, Sharon, directs him to a door that reads: *The Department of Code Enforcement.* Inside the door are rows of plain brown shelves filled with plain brown books. Carter rubs his hands together, rises to his toes, and pulls down several heavy hardcover books.

The codes he's in search of are online, yet woefully unorganized there, and Carter prefers the satisfaction of holding a clearly spelled-out building code in his hands: the weight and smell of the book, the indexes, the bullet points, the tables of contents. Carter spends so much time reading through the comfortingly clear rules and guidelines and ordinances and limitations and laws in a room without windows that evening falls without his noticing. He only realizes the late hour when Sharon asks if he needs to make any copies before she closes up for the night.

"That would be fantastic, Sharon. Thank you." Carter gathers a stack of books right up to his chin and follows Sharon to the copier behind her desk.

"I must say, it's not often that we get someone so enthusiastic about municipal codes in here." Sharon pushes a button and the copier rattles and wheezes to life.

Carter sets a book face down onto the first set of codes that will help him in his mission. "Some people just don't know how to have a good time, Sharon."

He leaves with a stack of papers neatly clipped and organized in a file folder; Sharon from The Department of Code Enforcement was so helpful! He writes exactly that on a comment card before taking the elevator back down and sends a text to Paige as he leaves City Hall. *Tell Eli to set up a meeting with the landlord ASAP.*

Paige sends back an emoji with question marks over its confused face, but this is too much information to explain via text, so Carter doesn't reply. He doesn't hear back from her for a few days, which is fine as he's bogged down in work and ongoing home repairs, and the message she finally sends is as vague and confusing as his probably was.

He's coming.

Carter is driving home from work. When he's stopped at a red light he texts back, asking for clarification. Paige replies, and Carter curses, making a U-turn at the next intersection.

The landlord. Now.

Eli and Paige meet him at the entrance of the warehouse under bright security lights, immediately demanding to know what is going on and what his grand plan is. Carter looks past them into the dark warehouse. "Where's Link?" A truck pulls up before anyone can answer.

"What's this about a sewage leak?"

Carter turns to Paige. "It was the only way to get him here," she says. Then she pinches the inside of Carter's arm. "You better know what the hell you're doing."

Carter nods, saying in a loud, bold voice and pointing to really sell it, "The sewage leak is you taking advantage of these hardworking artists."

A middle-aged man with a flat, serious face, wearing a polyester golf polo and creased khaki pants, steps into the halo of light. He looks at the three of them in turn, then says, "What?"

"Uh, thanks for coming by on such short notice, Mr. Reynolds." Eli shakes the landlord's hand. "We actually wanted to speak with you about the lease. I think? Carter?"

Carter clears his throat. He doesn't have his stack of papers with all the codes, and he only remembers some of them offhand. This is not how he imagined this going down, but he's here now. "Mr. Reynolds," Carter starts, his voice shakier than he'd like it to be. "Are you familiar with the property ordinances for the city of New Orleans as they pertain to tenants' rights?"

"Of course I am," Mr. Reynolds snaps. "I was in the middle of dinner; what is this?"

"Uh," Carter says, "This is, um."

Confused and panicked, Eli and Paige look at him. He really wishes Link were here; he's able to explain things with so much more confidence when Link is around.

"This is bullshit, then," Mr. Reynolds announces, then starts to walk away, out of the light. "Thanks for wasting my time."

"Wait!" Carter calls, searching his brain, *waste, waste water, water system... what was it?* "Chapter seventy... eight. Article, uh. Three! Section twenty-six dash... one one... one one... eight! 'The installation and repair of all plumbing and plumbing fixtures, um, must be inspected by the Board of New Orleans Governing Use of Sewage, Water and Drainage Systems.'" Carter inhales a gasping breath. "'Violations will be subject to fines and up to ninety days' imprisonment.'"

Mr. Reynolds steps back toward them, half under the security light and half out. "This some kind of a threat? You know I can just kick anyone out any time I want, right?"

Carter can hear the inward breaths Eli and Paige take and hold in unison. Carter swallows, smooths his hair and tie, and replies in a steadier voice. "No, sir. And no, you can't. Actually."

"What the hell do you think—" Mr. Reynolds takes a step toward Carter. So does Paige, protectively. Eli does too. Carter holds his hand up. He's got this; he remembers now. The neatly laid out codes flash like photos through his mind.

"Mr. Reynolds, as I'm sure you're aware, the New Orleans Code of Ordinances, Chapter Twenty-six: 'Buildings, Building Regulations and Housing Standards' details the requirements that landlords must adhere to, including but not limited to: Article Three, 'Plumbing.' Article Four, 'Minimum Property Maintenance Code.' Article Five, 'Minimum Standards for Certain Other Properties.' Article Six, 'Property Standards, General.'" Mr. Reynolds, Paige, and Eli stare at him as if he has four heads. Carter continues, more emphatically. "Article *Eight*, 'Minimum Standards for Parking Lots.' And skipping to Article Ten, 'Standards for Long-Term Rentals.' And that's not even getting into Chapter Seventy-four, 'Fire Prevention and Protection,' Chapter Seventy-eight, 'Floods and Flooding Damage,' and Chapter One Five Eight, 'Utilities.'"

Mr. Reynolds glares. "What is your point?"

"Well," Carter says, a smile creeping onto his face. "Looking around I see, offhand, a number of potential violations, all of them carrying fines and potential jail time. Of course, as you know all of this, I'm sure you've taken pains to adhere to the proper procedures for rectifying these violations through the relevant city boards and bureaus, and, as well, gotten all of these issues approved prior to renting out this property for commercial and residential use."

Mr. Reynolds crosses his arms. Paige and Eli start exchanging excited glances.

"You don't have to take my word for it," Carter adds, really getting into the game now. "You'll want to go to city hall. Take the second elevator, not the first, that one goes down to the parking garage, learned that the hard way. Second elevator, up to the seventh floor. At the seventh floor, you need to wait and be shown to a suite. *Inside* the suite, Sharon at the front desk—we're friends now, she'll vouch for me—will show you to the Department of Code Enforcement, which is a catalogue of books where all the codes I've referenced are written out. Go to the seventh shelf, third row from the top. Start with Chapter Twenty-six, Article One, Section two six dash one—"

"Okay!" Mr. Reynolds holds up both hands in surrender. "I can't listen to you yammer about codes and articles and elevators any longer. I have a ribeye waiting for me at home. I'll draw up a new one-year lease with the old rental amount, okay? Is that what you want?"

"No," Carter says, smug now, "we want a two-year lease at the same rate, with a provision for future rental adjustment percentages based on fair market value."

"Fine."

"Great. Eli?"

Eli blinks, looking back and forth at Carter and then Mr. Reynolds. "Uh. Yeah. Great."

"Great," Carter says again. "Enjoy that ribeye."

Mr. Reynolds shakes his head and steps back as if walking off a right hook to the jaw. Carter may not be tough or manly or macho, but he knows his building codes.

"You their lawyer or something?"

"No, sir." Carter puffs out his chest. "I'm an architect."

The landlord leaves, and Paige starts to squeal while Eli whacks Carter on the back. "How did you know he was in violation of all that stuff?" Eli says.

"Oh, I didn't." Carter laughs a little in relief. "Yeah, that whole thing could have really blown up in my face." He makes an explosion-like motion with his hands.

Eli shakes his head, laughing in the same relieved way. "I can't believe it."

"I can," Paige says, then pitches her voice to a shout, directing it to where Mr. Reynolds is getting into his truck. "Because no one is more pedantic than *my brother!*"

Taking it as a compliment, Carter smiles at Paige and Eli, who are swinging their clasped hands back and forth between them, and asks, "So where is Link?"

THIRTY-NINE

PAIGE AND ELI EXCHANGE A glance. "Wait, they didn't tell you?" Eli says. Paige releases his hand to grab Carter by the arm. "Let's go get a drink."

Carter moves his arm away. "Tell me what?" Eli and Paige look at each other again, having another one of those silent conversations, a terse one, until Carter can't take it anymore and says, "Someone tell me what is going on, *please.*"

Paige's head dips, and Eli answers, "Link left for Seattle a few hours ago."

"Oh." Carter nods. "Okay. Okay, that's fine." Forcing himself numb, he heads back to his car; the night falls around him as he steps away from the warehouse lights. Link left. Link left without saying a word to Carter. Not a goodbye. Not a *call you soon.* Nothing.

"Carter, don't go. Let's go grab a drink," Paige calls after him.

"Come on, my treat," Eli adds.

Carter shakes his head even though they probably can no longer see him. He was stupid to think that saving the warehouse would solve anything. Link was obviously eager to leave, and, yet again, no matter what Carter does, it will never be enough. He will never be enough. Footsteps crunch behind him, and Paige calls out to him, closer this time.

"I'll come hang out at your house. You shouldn't be alone right now."

"I'm fine," Carter snaps. She touches his arm again, and Carter wrenches it away. "Just leave me alone, Paige." He gets in his car, slams the door, revs the engine, and speeds out of the gravel lot, leaving Paige behind in clouds of dirt. He's fine. He's *fine.*

When he gets home, Carter drops into the camping chair in the living room and does something he never allowed himself after things ended with Matthew: He cries. A stopper finally uncorked, he cries angrily over Matthew and heartbroken over Link, sobs and hiccups despondently over the unfairness that he'll never get to have his own happily ever after while he watches everyone around him get theirs. Carter has never cared much about having the perfect home, the perfect job, the perfect life; these were the stifling parameters of his childhood, an illusion of perfection. All he wanted was someone who wanted him back, as is, flaws and insecurities and all. Carter really thought he'd found that. He really thought that he and Link would finally get things right.

His phone rings, probably Paige, then dings with a voicemail, probably Paige yelling at him to answer his damn phone. Carter goes upstairs to splash cold water on his blotchy face, dries off, and takes a few deep, shuddering breaths. He feels better for crying, a long-needed release. He should call Paige and take her up on that drink offer and apologize for the dirt clouds he left in his wake. Someone knocks on the door before he can finish dialing her number.

"I was just calling you—oh." It isn't Paige dropping by to badger him into not being alone, it's someone Carter doesn't know at all. They have blond hair cropped into a pixie cut, a silver nose ring, and eyes that dart nervously at Carter and not at Carter. It's a little late for solicitations, and they don't really *look* like a Jehovah's Witness or a Mormon in their pink cotton dress and whimsical silk scarf. Familiarity he can't place tugs at the back of his mind.

"Can I help you?"

"You're Carter, right?"

"Yes?" Carter answers, unsure if he should really be confirming his identity to this person who apparently knows him. "Do I know you?"

They hesitate, eyes darting again as if they also shouldn't be confirming who they are, then finally, "I'm Jamie. Um, can I come in?"

Carter robotically lets Jamie in, shows her to the dining room, and asks if she'd like something to drink. He goes to the fridge and grabs two bottles of sparkling water, then sits at the table that Link made with Link's ex-fiancée and Matthew's… whatever she is now. The last time he saw Jamie, he barely caught a glimpse of her: a blur of pink and purple ruffles, running off with his fiancé and away from her own wedding. Her hair was different too. He knows her but doesn't; he is connected to her in the strangest of ways. He has no social script for this situation whatsoever.

"I'm sorry, I know this must be so completely awkward and uncomfortable for you," Jamie says after a stretch of long, awkward, and uncomfortable silence.

"Um," Carter replies. "Well…" He takes a drink of water.

Jamie doesn't open hers. "You don't owe me any time at all, for good reason," she says, "So I'll cut to the chase: I don't think Matthew is over you."

Carter chokes on his mouthful of fizzing water. After he stops coughing and cleans up the dribbles on his chin and the table, he croaks, "What?"

Jamie's hands spread flat on the table; her face is pulled tight. "I just," Jamie starts, looking at her hands. "We're supposed to move to Austin together, somewhere new where we can start over. But lately Matt's been dragging his feet, making up excuses for why he has to keep delaying things. Delaying us. And—" She looks up, eyes flashing with hurt. "The other night I found him going through some pictures of you two. So I came here. I didn't know who else to talk to."

Reeling, Carter can only think to ask, "How did you even find me?" Matthew doesn't know where he is, and Link said that they'd made a clean break with Jamie, so it must somehow be because of—

"Your sister," Jamie says, confirming what Carter had just figured out was the connection. "I'm still friends with Eli on Facebook, and Paige tags him in stuff all the time, including some photos of your house, with a geotag. Honestly, it's way too easy to track people down these days."

Carter wouldn't know; he thought that sort of thing would be inappropriate and invasive. "I don't really understand what you want from me." His tone is terse because it's late and he's tired and sad and really believed he was through with all of this.

Jamie looks down, cowed. "I have no right to ask you for anything. It's been so much harder than I thought, moving forward with Matt. I guess I thought we'd just fall back into it, that it would be easier. I hurt Link for this. I disappointed my family, and my friends think I'm crazy. Maybe I just need someone to tell me that I haven't made a huge mistake."

What Carter should do is send her on her way, because she's right, he doesn't owe her anything. But what has his bitterness ever gotten him? And if he can't get his happily ever after, then he can at least help Jamie and Matthew find theirs. If this is his lot in life, so be it.

"Look, I can't tell you that you didn't make a mistake with Matthew," Carter starts. Jamie nods, lips pressed tightly together. "But," Carter continues, "he did drag me halfway across the country on the off chance that the person he never stopped being in love with for a moment in the course of an entire decade *might* still love him back, confessing his feelings at your wedding, even. And you came all the way here to talk to ֺne because you're so afraid of losing him. I can tell you honestly that no one has ever done anything close to that for me." It's sad but true, and probably no one ever will. There's no point dwelling on it. "That sort of love, I think, is worth fighting for."

Jamie's smile is sad, but maybe a little hopeful. "I think so too."

Carter tips his head in acknowledgment. "And, if it helps him to move on, you can tell Matthew that when he confessed why we were in New Orleans, that he'd come to win you back, I was relieved. Not angry or sad. Relieved. We weren't really happy, and he can stop feeling guilty about it. Matthew doesn't still have feelings for me; he just hates that I wouldn't let him smooth everything over so we could both move on." Carter lifts his hands from his lap and waves them in an arc. "I release him. You have my blessing. For real."

Jamie reaches across the table and takes both of his hands in hers. "Thank you. You are everything Matt said you were and more." Carter blinks, staring at Jamie's hands. "I hope you find happiness, Carter."

She stands, and Carter watches, still trying to grasp what just happened. It's stupid: not what Jamie's said, but the way he's been acting. *I hope you find happiness* echoes in his brain as he walks Jamie to the door, as if happiness is a stray penny on the sidewalk, waiting for him to accidentally stumble upon it. That isn't the way happiness works.

"I wish there was some way I could repay you for your kindness," Jamie says on his darkened porch. Carter takes other people's whims and hopes and makes them real. He does not wait around for happy accidents.

"Actually, could you drop me off at the airport?"

FORTY

"Please remove laptops from bags and place shoes in a separate bin!"

Carter shuffles through the security line already in his socks with his items neatly arranged in two bins, annoyed that the person in front of him is yakking on their phone instead of paying attention and following the security protocol. They're going to make everyone wait longer, and Carter just spent a small fortune on a last-minute ticket to Seattle. He's going to be so irritated if he misses his flight.

"Please remove laptops from bags and place shoes in a separate bin!"

Carter glares at the back of the person in front of him. *Do it.*

"Carter!"

Do it. Do it, do it, do it, do it. Do. It.

"Carter Jacob!"

Carter shuffles forward, looking around. He could have sworn he heard his name. He slides his bins onto the rollers for the X-ray machine and waits to be scanned. He hears his name again, and movement catches his eye. Link? Just past security and into the terminal, Link stands on tiptoe, waving their hands to get Carter's attention.

"Carter! Don't—"

"Please remove laptops from bags and place shoes in a separate bin!"

Whatever Link was about to say is drowned out by the announcement, and then the person in front of him finally catches a clue and starts to frantically dump their carry-on while simultaneously trying to remove their shoes and get into the scanning line. Carter glances at them disdainfully. When he looks back, Link is gone.

He gets through security and claims his things, going immediately to where Link was with his shoes tucked under one arm and his bag still open. Not there. Did he imagine them? Carter shoves his feet into his shoes and gets his bag situated, then turns to scour the terminal in search of Link, provided he was not, in fact, hallucinating. He is *very* tired. And then he spots them on the *other* side of the security line.

"Link!"

"Carter?"

"Link?"

"Carter!"

Link says something that's drowned out by another announcement, so Carter rushes to the exit, winding through the terminal and people, out past the signs that shout *NO RE-ENTRY,* and quickly makes his way to the spot where Link just was—and is no longer. Carter hikes his bag up higher on his shoulder, pants for breath, and spins in place. Where the hell did they go? Someone bumps into him—

"Link?"

"Excuse me, sorry."

Not Link. Carter huffs out a frustrated breath. This is ridiculous. Link was just here. Someone else bumps into him, and Carter ignores them. Did Link go through security to meet Carter in the terminal? Should he buy another ticket and get in line again? The person who bumped into him taps his shoulder. Okay, he's sort of in the way, but there's plenty of room to maneuver around him—

"Oh. Link!"

"Carter!" Link reaches for him, then stops and brushes a lock of hair from their face. "What are you doing here?"

Carter shakes his head. "Me? What are you doing here? I thought you were in Seattle."

"I was. I mean I was going to." Link is dressed in all black: textured pants and a long shirt slit open on the sides, black boots, a round-brimmed black hat, black eyeliner, black nail polish. Something one might wear in Seattle. "Where were you going?"

Carter flattens his hair nervously before answering, "Seattle." He had this whole speech planned. He was going to show up at Link's door and proclaim that he's figured it all out, he knows exactly how he and Link can make things work; it was going to be very compelling and well-thought-out and romantic too. Only, he was going to plan that speech on the long overnight flight to Seattle. Now that he's suddenly standing in front of Link, he doesn't know what to say.

"I went to your house," Link says. "But you weren't there. Paige said you might be here."

How did she know? "Oh," Carter says.

"You were going to Seattle for me?"

Carter nods. "You didn't go to Seattle for me?"

"Yes." Link bites their bottom lip. "I, uh, I had this whole speech. But now that I've been saying it over and over in my head for a while, it sounds stupid."

Carter nods. "Okay."

Once again, he and Link find themselves at an impasse. The airport rushes busily around them, with people who know exactly where to go and what they need to do to get there. Link hesitates, so Carter hesitates, then can't help it and blurts, "I don't know how to make us make sense. We haven't done anything in order or according to the steps we're supposed to follow, and I don't think that's something we can change." There is no such thing as starting over, not really, and he and Link will always have come from rubble.

Link glances down. "I know. I know we can't."

"No," Carter says. "However." Link's eyes meet his again, and, just like the first time, on a day that should have sent them on opposite paths yet somehow brought him and Link together, Link's gaze connects to something deep and unexplainable inside of Carter, something that's the opposite of pragmatic and sensible. "We don't need our story or our past to make sense, because you and me. We do. We make sense."

Link smiles, briefly, and then shakes their head. "Carter, you need more than that. You need a solid foundation and, and a logical procession of steps. I know you."

"If you really knew me," Carter says, blunt, "then you would know that I'm also drawn to things that are beautiful just for their own sake, even if I don't always understand them, even if they don't always make sense." A logical order of relationship steps is what he had before, and thank god Matthew was brave enough to risk his heart on something real and save them both.

Link's head tilts. "Are you saying I don't always make sense, Carter Jacob?"

Carter looks up, glancing around as if in thought. He smiles. "Yes."

Link scowls playfully, then laughs. "All right. Fair enough." Carter wishes he and Link weren't in public right now; he would have liked Link showing up on his doorstep with a speech they'd thought up just for him. He would have really liked bringing Link inside and kissing them soundly afterward. As if reading his mind, which is ridiculous, of course, Link takes a deep breath and says, "I'm gonna do my dumb speech now."

Link's eyes close and they say in a rehearsed rush, "Carter. I know you don't believe in fate, but I do. Because I know that meeting you was my destiny. That night after I was left at the altar, sitting at that bar all alone, I was convinced that that was the end of my story, the end of my happiness. But it wasn't." Their eyes open, green and gold in the bright airport lights. "It was a beginning. It was something that wasn't supposed to be real but was, from the very start. I hate that you've moved on. I was so wrong; I am miserable without you. And I swear to you, Carter Jacob, that I am going to figure out how to be the person that you need me to be, because I'm in love with you. I have been for a long time."

Carter can't move, can't speak, can't think, can't breathe. Link loves him. Link is in love with him and has been for a long time. Link wants to be with him. Link is with him. Right now. Here. Carter blinks and blinks and says, "Can we go?"

It pours down rain on the cab ride back from the airport. In the backseat, Link takes Carter's hand, and Carter threads his fingers securely through Link's.

"You love me?" Carter asks, needing to hear it again.

Link smiles, soft and secretive. "Yes."

Carter presses his leg against Link's, hip to thigh to knee to ankle; desire thrums at every point of contact. At Carter's house, they splash through puddles together and laugh and try not to laugh too loudly because it's late at night now. Carter's ribs feel as if they've been cracked wide open, that beams of light pour from him as he kisses Link just inside and against the front door and in the living room and the kitchen, then stumbling around the dining room and tripping up the stairs to bang into his bedroom.

"Link," Carter says, his back pushed up against his bedroom door. He whispers the words over and over into Link's throat and mouth, gasps them into the room as Link sinks down in front of him and starts to unbuckle his belt: "I love you."

"I love you, too," Link looks up with one mischievous eyebrow raised, fingers poised over the button on Carter's pants. "May I?"

Carter's head thunks back against the door. "Yes," he answers on a quick inhalation. "Yes, please."

FORTY-ONE

LINK TAKES CARTER INTO THEIR mouth without any further preamble. Carter is still in rain-damp clothes, and Link is still in a jaunty black hat. Link's head moves achingly slow, a drag of lips, a flicker of tongue, so gentle, so slow. It's not even foreplay, it's whatever comes before that, like the *click click click* of a gas stove trying to light. Carter can't get a single breath; his lungs are seizing. Then Link sucks him in earnest, once, then twice, and Carter, shuddering, gasps. Link pulls away entirely, stands to kiss Carter, and sucks on his tongue again.

Link sinks back down to a kneeling position.

"Oh, god," Carter says, shivering and pulsing with need.

Link's answering grin is dangerously pleased. "How long can you hold out, do you think?" A tease of lips, a swirl of tongue.

A second, Carter thinks. *Forever. Somewhere in between.* "I don't know," he answers, then asks, "How long do you need me to?" Link's head bobs deeply, taking Carter down to the hot clasp of their soft palate.

Link pulls back and coughs, answering, voice rough. "I guess we're about to find out."

So Carter floats and floats, lost to the mellow, easy pleasure. There is only Link's warm, wet mouth and Link's softly grabbing hands, one on Carter's belly and one on his thigh. Link huffs short little breaths, and Carter moans long, rumbling ones. When his moans get too loud, too wanting, when Carter's fingernails scrabble on the wood holding him upright, somehow, still, Link pulls off, stands, and presses their mouth to Carter's lips.

He's resigned himself to this blissful purgatory where orgasms don't exist when Link sits back, rubbing at their jaw and saying, "Okay, my knees hurt, damn."

Link hops over to the bed and drops down, the mattress bouncing with their enthusiasm. Carter, however, can't move at all for fear his legs will give out beneath him. Link crosses their legs primly, shrugs their shoulders and smirks, one shoulder coyly lifted. "This is fun."

Carter laughs, and it's enough to break the spell so he can at least walk on wobbly legs to the bed. "Torturing me is fun?"

"Oh, absolutely."

Carter flips Link's hat off, then crawls on top of them, captures Link's swollen lips in another kiss, and nudges them back and up higher on the bed. Carter starts to lie down, then grunts at the feel of his damp clothes bunched against his skin and wriggles free of the pants and shirt and briefs. Link watches with blatant desire, until Carter says, "Your turn," and moves back on top. He finds the spot on Link's neck that smells heady and sweet, where Link's pulse taps against his tongue. The sides of their shirt are open to the bottom curve of Link's ribcage, and Carter slides his knuckles up and up until he finds where Link's nipples are stiff and hard. In the same gentle tease, Carter circles the nubs, flicks his thumb in a just-there touch. He pushes the shirt aside, fabric bunching in his hand against Link's sternum, and then teases with his tongue just as he had with his fingers and thumb.

When Link's hips start to buck, back arching, mouth dropping open, Carter's plan for slow-spooling revenge spirals out of control, his own arousal coming to the forefront, his body reaching, desperately aching. Link gasps, back bowing, and Carter's bottom teeth scrape on a nipple. Link's hips grind and thrust and roll against Carter's hips.

Carter rolls away, onto his back. "I'm gonna come."

Link, more winded than they were after a sprint through the rain and tumble through the house, simply says, "Okay." But then they strip off their shirt and pants and shimmy out of green striped underwear and stretch languorously, all dark eyes and curved mouth and moonlit skin, on Carter's new flower-print duvet. They are so beautiful Carter's lungs struggle again for one single breath.

Carter shifts to his side, curving his body over Link's. His jaw is sore now, too, his lips are tingly-numb, and the need to come is sharp in his belly. Link hikes a leg over Carter's hip, their knee rests on the small of Carter's back and ankle on the back of his thigh, encouraging Carter's body down, down, and over until he's lined up just right. Carter cups Link's face in both hands and moves against them, mouths pressed together but not really kissing, just breathing. He can't tell who comes first because they're both shaking and moaning, falling together; the intense bright light in Carter's chest reaches out to Link until he's wrung out and panting.

He sleeps for a while, he thinks, or at least some measure of time has passed without Carter noticing. Body sticky and mouth dry, he retrieves a warm washcloth from the bathroom and two cold sparkling waters from the kitchen, not bothering with a robe as he normally would, even though he now lives alone. Link has the sheet pulled up to their waist when Carter gets back; their eyes and limbs are heavy with sleep as they take a water.

"Thanks."

"Mmhmm." Carter takes several long, quenching gulps.

"Carter?" Link takes a sip of theirs and then sets it aside. "I need to tell you something."

"All right." Carter finishes his drink, hiding a burp as he tosses the can aside. He's usually politer after sex, but then he's never really had sex quite as brazenly desperate as this. He tucks himself back into bed; the sheet settles around the shapes of both of their bodies.

Link turns to the side, face pressed into the pillow. "That very first night we met. When we were both a little—"

"Completely wasted?" Carter fills in. He still hardly remembers anything, which is a shame because it was his first night with Link, his first night in New Orleans. It clearly has had a lasting impact.

"Right," Link says. "The night we met and got a little completely wasted." Link's nose scrunches; their shoulders wiggle them higher on the bed. "That night we got a tarot reading, and after that… after that, you kissed me."

Carter's head lifts from the pillow. "Oh. Wow, that's so inappropriate. Link, I'm sorry. I don't really remember, but I'm sorry. That was crossing the line."

"That's the thing, though." Link pulls the sheet higher. "I wanted you to. I mean, I did but I didn't and I was definitely flirting, but just as a fun distraction, I thought, and that was all and then—it was actually amazing. Like, the rest of the world froze, and you were the only thing that existed." Carter can't stop a smile at that, but Link shakes their head. "I'm sure you can imagine how much that freaked me out, since I was supposed to be married to someone else that night."

"Oh." Carter's head flops back onto the pillow. "Yeah."

"So when I asked you to stay," Link continues, "It was partly because I liked you but mostly because I was hoping you'd turn out to be an asshole and I could forget about you. You turned out to be even sweeter and more wonderful than I could have ever anticipated."

Carter purses his lips. "Sorry?"

Link shoves at his chest. "You should be. You made me fall in love with you. Jerk."

Carter catches Link's hand, slips his fingers between Link's and puts their joined hands on his own stomach. "Even then?" he asks.

"Even then," Link says. "I wasn't trying to be confusing. I just needed some time."

"I felt that way too," Carter confesses. "That must be why I kept that card."

Link shifts next to him. "Card?"

Carter quickly runs downstairs to where the little birdhouse cottage sits on his mantel above his new wood-burning stove. He kept all the souvenirs from his vacation and fake honeymoon inside, including the tarot card.

"Any idea how I got this?" Carter says, handing it to Link and turning on his bedside light. The card is yellow, orange, and blue, with a person holding a bag on a stick, standing on a cliff under a golden sun that's either rising or setting, clearly about to embark on a harebrained journey. *The Fool.* He doesn't believe in fortune-telling or tarot cards any more than he believes in ghosts and magical herbs and fate, yet he's kept it this whole time, as if it had the ability to keep him connected to Link, as if it meant something.

"I don't remember you taking it," Link says. "But the reading... I think it was about a new journey and a new opportunity on the horizon and having faith in it." Link huffs a laugh. "I do remember you saying how silly that was, that drawing a card is chance, as mystical as flipping a coin." Yes, that does sound like him.

Carter takes the card back. Lucky guesses, but some of that did come true. Or he made it come true. Does it matter, choice or fate, if he ended up here? *Having faith.* He can do that. And he doesn't need Link to change their dreams or be someone else for him, even if that means keeping faith that he and Link will have to find a way back to each other, eventually. He can't be afraid of letting Link go, or of loneliness, or of the uncertainty of the rest of this journey with Link going forward. Foolish? Perhaps.

"Link," Carter asks. "What was in Seattle?"

FORTY-TWO

IN THE TEN WEEKS SINCE Link left, Carter has been splitting his attention between projects at work, time out with coworkers, regular lunches and manicures with Paige, visiting with neighbors, watching Saints games at Eli's, and putting some finishing touches on his house: replacing lighting fixtures, adding ornamentation to the outside, installing new window treatments, replacing the handles on cabinets and doors, finally getting the yard in shape. He stays busy enough that he shouldn't have time to miss Link very much.

He does.

On the Saturdays that there aren't any afternoon football games, Carter revisits some of the places he went with Link on their fake honeymoon: the park with the wind chime tree, Bourbon Street, which is quite a different experience during the day, the French Market, the trolley to the restaurant with po'boys twice, the graveyard tour, and the Garden District tour thrice. He hasn't gone back to the hotel, though he's passed nearby. It feels too sacred.

He even takes a singles cooking class at the school near the river, though he feels a little silly at first. He learns how to make coq au vin blanc and seared duck breast with cherry port reduction, though, which makes him feel fancy. He plans on making both for an upcoming, very romantic dinner date he's had planned for quite some time.

Two more weeks.

Tonight, he's having a bowl of ramen with seasoning packet reduction after rushing home and changing quickly. The weather has become mild again, and the new energy-saving, storm-impact-resisting windows in the dining room are open to a cool evening breeze as Carter eats in front of his open laptop, detailing the last house project he's been busy with between scoops of noodles. "I went to the salvage yard like you said, and they did have several vintage doors; you were right. This one needs some patching, but otherwise I just need to take a little steel wool to it and then stain and finish it with a natural oil. Not too much. Really keep the worn, vintage look."

On the screen, all the way from Seattle, Link listens, chin propped on one hand, adorably cuddled up in a blanket. "Hmm, what kind of oil?"

Carter sets the spoon against the bowl to think. "Tung seem to be the recommended one. Maybe I'll go out on a limb and do walnut, though."

Link leans closer to the screen, winking saucily. "Gettin' wild without me, huh?"

Carter grins. "Anyway, enough about wood staining. What did you learn at school at today?" It's actually a highly coveted, very competitive artist residency, which Carter and Link agreed was a once-in-a-lifetime opportunity Link couldn't pass up. Not for Carter's sake. Carter had a fully refundable ticket that he cancelled, using the credits to get Link to Seattle as soon as possible. Carter has faith in Link and faith in this relationship. He's not afraid of being alone anymore. He doesn't *like* it, but he's not afraid of it. Still, he tucked the tarot card into a pocket on Link's backpack before they boarded the plane, like a talisman keeping him connected until Link returns. It's ridiculous, but Link brings out a less pragmatic side of him.

"I think today I mastered my old nemesis, clay pots. I made one that *doesn't* look like someone sat on it and then kicked it down some stairs and then sat on it again." Link moves around their tiny artist's dorm to show Carter clay pots lined on a shelf. The point of doing the program is to give Link time to focus solely on art, as well as make connections and experiment with new things. Carter had no issue going the whole twelve weeks without seeing Link, letting them be totally immersed in the program, but Link surprised him with a plane ticket to Seattle about five weeks in for a weekend. Carter *loves* Seattle now.

"Amazing," Carter says, because they are. He reaches for the lumpy, sagging clay pot filled with old wilted herbs that lives on the dining room table. "I still like this one best, though."

Link's laugh comes trilling through the speaker. "You do not."

"I do so," Carter defends. "It's my most prized possession."

"More than the table I spent countless sleepless nights getting absolutely perfect?" Link says, expression stern but lips twitching with a smile.

"Eh, it's okay." Carter teases back. "I never told you; I found the flower."

Now Link does smile, wide and bright. "I knew you would. I still have it, the flower you gave me on that picnic." Link sighs happily. "It was incredible."

Carter sets his chin on his folded hands and sighs. "I know. Those goat cheese crostini? Life-changing."

"I'm hanging up on you," Link says, and the picture on the screen swoops down as if Link is closing the laptop in indignation.

"No wait," Carter calls out, laughing. "Don't leave me!"

Link's smiling face appears back on the screen. "Never."

As hard as it has been, being away from Link, Carter hasn't had a moment of doubt, never worries that Link is in danger of slipping through his fingers like water, running faster the harder he tries to hold on. He never wants Link to feel as if they have to rush things or be afraid of taking time apart. Carter isn't going anywhere. He and Link have all the time in the world.

One week before Link is due back in New Orleans, Carter takes the Haunted New Orleans tour again. He has a different tour guide this time: Pierre, who has an impressively bushy mustache and likes to emphasize the history behind each place. That part Carter likes. He finds it easier to pay attention, but that's probably because last time he was distracted by Link's arm looped through his and Link's hip brushing his own, and how desperately he was trying to tamp down his feelings while failing spectacularly.

The tour starts at a voodoo shop at night, hits the haunted pharmacy and hospital and the same restaurants and bars. Someone claims to see a face in a window and another swears they feel a cold presence. The closest Carter comes to a disturbing encounter is when his stomach rumbles as the tour winds through a dark alleyway where a grisly murder took place hundreds of years ago. "Sorry," Carter says, when the group turns to look at him. The crawfish étouffée at the last so-called haunted restaurant smelled divine. "Stomach ghost," he jokes. No one in the group seems to find it funny. When he tells the story later over video chat, Link laughs brightly.

"I went upstairs at that same bar where you tried to scare me—"

"Did scare you," Link corrects. "And it wasn't me, it was a ghost."

Carter's eyes roll. "Well, your ghost friend wasn't there."

Link is tinkering with something offscreen, using a tiny pair of pliers to shape something that must be rather small. "Must only feel comfortable using me as conduit," Link comments. "You know, Danielle claims I have *the gift*."

Carter *mmhmms* skeptically. These days he does believe in the metaphysical more than he used to; he has no other way to explain how he feels about Link and how they found each other, how they keep finding each other. It defies logic because it's far bigger. It's still fun to mess with Link about it, though. "Okay, use your gift and tell me what you see." Carter leans close, closer, so his eyes are level with the little camera circle and his face takes up the entire screen.

"That's easy," Links says. "I see my future."

EPILOGUE

IT'S TRUE WHAT THEY SAY about Texas; everything is bigger. In fact, Carter gets lost on his way back from the bathroom, having crossed a vast field of wildflowers to get there, but on the return trip, he's apparently crossed a different meadow and ended up at an entirely different barn. He's worried he left the wedding venue altogether, but, when he looks around, Carter can see the other barn at the other end of the property, with the homestead positioned between.

He should go back. It's quiet in this barn, though, unlike the other one. And the building is interesting. By the time he makes it back to the correct barn, the ice in his drink has completely melted, and he seems to have missed the cake-cutting.

"Hey, did you wander off?" Eli greets him first, loudly over the music, with his arm resting around Paige's waist.

Paige, even louder, says, "Remember how Mom got you a backpack with a leash on it?" She turns to Eli. "He had to use it until he was like, seven." She laughs. Carter scowls. He was five when he stopped using that stupid thing. *Maybe* six.

"Where did you go?" Link hands him a fresh drink: a mint julep. Carter takes a sip and smiles over the rim, ignoring Paige.

"Well, there's another barn. I think it was a horse stable, actually, given the shape and structure of the building and its positioning on the property." He gestures excitedly; a little of his drink splashes out. "It looks as if the stone walls on the perimeter are original; they have to be a least a hundred years old if I'm recognizing the stonework accurately."

Link pecks Carter's cheek. "Ugh, you could not be cuter if you tried."

Carter's cheek tingles when Link moves away. He agonized over whether this wedding was a good idea, though he is glad for the excuse to spend so much uninterrupted time with Link, who is looking at him with their eyes cast low and mouth quirked up. *How soon is too soon to politely leave a reception?*

Paige interrupts, directing an eye-roll at Link. "You find the strangest things charming about him." And in her blunt but loving Paige way, she adds with an approving nod, "I'm glad someone does."

The slow, romantic song that was Jamie and Matthew's first dance as a married couple switches to something upbeat enough to groove to, and Eli drags Link off to dance, leaving Paige and Carter to sit at the white-linen-covered table with two of Jamie's coworkers. So far it's mostly been folksy piano music intercut with folksy guitar music at the reception. Matthew never listened to folk music, so he no doubt let Jamie pick their wedding soundtrack. Carter feels strange knowing that and stranger still being here and watching them say their vows and promise each other a forever.

"It's weird for you, right?" Paige says, never one to leave things alone.

"It's fine," Carter says without thinking, which makes Paige give him a sharp sidelong glance. Carter tries again, replying honestly, "Yeah, it's weird."

Paige, who is watching Eli dance and sipping an appletini, nods. She netted an invitation to the wedding by becoming fast friends with Jamie over social media, as only Paige can do. "Is it, like, closure, at least?"

"Nah," Carter says. Paige gives him a look again, but he's not being dishonest. "I got closure a long time ago. I'm okay, really." Carter's left thumb moves to touch his ring finger on the same hand in what has become a habitual gesture in the last few months since he's had a ring there, one Link designed and crafted in Seattle. It has a tiny intricate filigree design, like the wrought iron gates back home that Carter loves so much. Link restaged their first picnic together, with the same carriage ride, same blanket, and same food; Carter was so delighted he didn't even notice Link had gone to one knee. A year or so officially together, not on a specific date or under a certain timeline, beneath the wind chime tree, Carter said yes. Link confessed that they had been waiting in agony to ask him for months, though it seemed a tad soon to Carter, so in that way it was perfect timing for both of them.

After three up-tempo songs, another slow one cues up. Much of the crowd gathers at the far end of the barn, where fairy lights are strung in a circle. Eli comes to Paige for a dance and Carter finds himself tugged into Link's longer frame, tucked in close with his face buried in Link's neck.

"Having fun?" Link's arms hold Carter snug around the shoulders.

"Sure," Carter says.

"You want to go look at that old barn again, don't you?"

Carter's smile curves against Link's skin. "Yes."

He and Link sneak out, running across the fields of wildflowers while holding hands. A warm Texas breeze lifts Carter's sport coat and musses his hair, while Link's gray kilt lifts too high, exposing their strong thighs. Inside the stable, Carter doesn't look around at all, but turns immediately to the only thing he cares about doing right now: cupping Link's face in both hands and kissing them soundly.

Link says, blinking slowly, "That is not what I had in mind, but I do like the way you think, Carter Jacob."

Carter thinks of sliding his palm up Link's thigh, right under the drape of the kilt's fluttering skirt to the snug black briefs beneath, then under those too. He doesn't, because they're both too unsettled with the strangeness of the situation, and because the stables haven't entirely lost the lingering smell of horse. There's also a hotel to go back to, without the threat of a wedding guest one of them might know walking in.

Making eye contact with Matthew's mother as Jamie came down the aisle, for example, was an unpleasant moment Carter wishes they both could have avoided.

"Is this weird for you?"

Link's head tilts. "Making out in a horse stable? Eh, it's not the first time." Carter laughs, and Link says more seriously, "It's… less weird than I thought it would be?"

"Yeah," Carter says. "I get that."

Jamie called Carter personally before sending him an invitation, insisting that it was only because of Carter that she and Matthew got past the initial turmoil and were still together and getting married, and of course Carter had to come to the wedding. And who else would he bring but Link? Though he was okay with going by himself, if Link needed him to.

"When Jamie started to walk down the aisle," Link says, toying with the collar of Carter's sport coat, "I was back there for second, waiting at the other end. And when it was me, then, I just—I knew something wasn't right. That the way I felt wasn't the way you should feel when someone is walking down the aisle to you." Link's hands move to fret with Carter's tie, and Carter covers their hands with his own. "The way Matthew looked at her…"

"Yeah," Carter says. "That's the way you look at someone when you know—"

"It's right," Link fills in, holding Carter's gaze for a long, meaningful moment, then sighs and says, "So are we gonna make out in this barn or what?"

"Is there a significant difference, do you think, between a barn and a stable? I'd venture that a stable refers to a building specifically built for livestock, while—"

"Okay," Link steps back with a wry grin. "We're talking about this stable instead. You are so lucky you're cute."

Walking with hands clasped and footsteps echoing on the stone floor, Carter points out interesting architectural details, and Link admires the handcrafted ironwork on the windows and doors, explaining how it was created. The high, pitched roof looks entirely rebuilt, and it's clear where the stones had to be filled in, and where the dark stains of overgrown vegetation couldn't be completely washed away. The process of saving and refurbishing the old building must have been tedious and enormously challenging; certainly bulldozing it and starting over would have been an easy call for most contractors.

Someone must have seen something worth keeping in this forgotten place: a second chance, another chapter, a beginning where others would have seen an ending.

"We should get married here," Link says, fingers trailing the bricks of a low window; some old, some new. "It suits us."

Carter stops, shakes his head. "No." Link stops too, surprised. "I mean, I love the mix of old and new, the ironwork and how sturdy the building is and how much sense it makes here, but it's not us." Link's eyebrows pull together; a little crease forms between. Carter goes up on his toes and kisses it, taking a breath in and out with his lips still pressed to Link's forehead.

He pulls back enough to see Link's eyes, and his breath catches at the way Link looks at him, as if Carter is somehow the amazing one. "You and me," Carter says. "We're something new." He and Link needed the past to find each other, but they don't need the lingering fingerprints of other people's stories on their hearts as they move forward together. Carter and Link aren't the castoffs at all.

They are the meant-to-be.

ACKNOWLEDGMENTS

THANK YOU TO ANNIE, CANDY, and CB for believing in this story, and in my ability to tell it.

To my family for their endless patience and support, and my Interlude Press author family for being so incredibly talented and kind; you all inspire me.

ABOUT THE AUTHOR

Lilah Suzanne is a queer author of Amazon bestseller *Broken Records*, part of the Spotlight series along with *Burning Tracks* and *Blended Notes*. Lilah also authored *Spice*, the novellas *Pivot & Slip* and *After the Sunset*, and the short story *Halfway Home*, which was featured in the holiday anthology *If the Fates Allow*. A writer from a young age, Lilah resides in North Carolina and mostly enjoys staying indoors, though sometimes ventures out for concerts, museum visits, and quiet walks in the woods.

interlude**press**™

interludepress.com
@InterludePress
interludepress
store.interludepress.com

interlude  press
also by Lilah Suzanne...

Broken Records
Spotlight Series, Book One

Los Angeles-based stylist Nico Takahashi loves his job—or at least, he used to. Feeling fed up and exhausted from the cutthroat, gossip-fueled business of Hollywood, Nico daydreams about packing it all in and leaving for good. So when Grady Dawson—sexy country music star and rumored playboy—asks Nico to style him, Nico is reluctant. But after styling a career-changing photo shoot, Nico follows Grady to Nashville where he finds it increasingly difficult to resist Grady's charms.

ISBN (print) 978-1-941530-57-3 | (eBook) 978-1-941530-58-0

Burning Tracks
Spotlight Series, Book Two

In the sequel to *Broken Records*, Gwen Pasternak has it all: a job she loves as a celebrity stylist and a beautiful wife, Flora. But as her excitement in working with country music superstar Clementine Campbell grows, Gwen second-guesses her quiet domestic bliss. Meanwhile, her business partner, Nico Takahashi and his partner, reformed bad-boy musician Grady Dawson, face uncertainties of their own.

ISBN (print) 978-1-941530-99-3 | (eBook) 978-1-945053-00-9

Blended Notes
Spotlight Series, Book Three

Grady Dawson is at the top of his music career and planning his wedding with boyfriend Nico when his past shows up, news of his nuptials is leaked, and his record company levels impossible demands. Can he make the ultimate choice between a private life with Nico and the public demands of his career?

ISBN (print) 978-1-945053-23-8 | (eBook) 978-1-945053-40-5

"Halfway Home"
An Interlude Press Short Story featured in If the Fates Allow

Avery Puckett has begun to wonder if her life has become joyless. One night, fate intervenes in the form of a scraggly dog shivering and alone in a parking lot. Avery takes him to a nearby shelter called Halfway Home where she meets bright and beautiful Grace, who is determined to save the world one stray at a time.

ISBN (print) 978-1-945053-47-4 | ISBN (eBook) 978-1-945053-48-1

"After the Sunset"
An Interlude Press Short Story

Caleb Harris and Ty Smith-Santos have never crossed paths until they learn that a farm in Sunset Hallow, Washington has been bequeathed to both of them. They prepare to sell the farmhouse, but soon find themselves falling for the charming farm, the lonely man who left it to them, and each other..

ISBN (eBook) 978-1-945053-49-8

Spice

In his Ask Eros advice column, Simon Beck has an answer to every relationship question his readers can throw at him. But in his life, the answers are a little more elusive—until he meets the newest and cutest member of his company's computer support team. Simon may be charmed, but will Benji help him answer the one relationship question that's always stumped him: how to know he's met Mr. Right?

ISBN (print) 978-1-941530-25-2 | (eBook) 978-1-941530-26-9

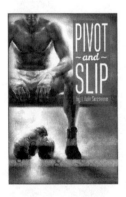

Pivot and Slip

Former Olympic hopeful Jack Douglas traded competitive swimming for professional yoga and never looked back. When handsome pro boxer Felix Montero mistakenly registers for his yoga for Seniors class, Jack takes an active interest both in Felix's struggles to manage stress and in his heart and discovers along the way that he may have healing of his own to do.

ISBN (print) 978-1-941530-03-0 | (eBook) 978-1-941530-12-2